A MATTER
OF PRINCIPLE

A Novel

A MATTER OF PRINCIPLE

A Novel

Susan Beth Pfeffer

Delacorte Press/New York

Published by
Delacorte Press
1 Dag Hammarskjold Plaza
New York, N.Y. 10017

I wish to thank Leo Pfeffer, Alan Pfeffer, and
Christy Emanuel for their help with the legal aspects
of this book, and Freda Pfeffer for her help with
everything else.

Manufactured in the United States of America

First printing

Designed by Richard Oriolo

Library of Congress Cataloging in Publication Data

Pfeffer, Susan Beth [date of birth]
A matter of principle.

Summary: A group of high school students are suspended
from school for publishing an underground newspaper that
the principal finds objectionable.
[1. School stories.   2. Journalism—Fiction.
3. Liberty of the press—Fiction]   I. Title.
PZ7.P44855Mat   [Fic]   81-15288
ISBN 0-440-05612-8   AACR2

P475m

For
Peggy & Lisa Lakin

ONE

"But it's an important issue!" Melissa said a little louder than she probably should have. I lifted my head up from the copy I was editing and looked at her confronting Miss Holdstein.

As far as I knew, Miss Holdstein had never lost a confrontation, and I doubted this was going to be the first time. She gave Melissa a withering look and said, "Correcting school policy is not the function of the school newspaper."

"We're not correcting!" Melissa cried, and then looked a little embarrassed. "We're suggesting. We're making an editorial comment. We're doing what newspapers are supposed to do. We're trying to get people to think."

I looked around the classroom where we were putting the *Southfield Sentinel* together. Most of the kids were looking straight ahead at Miss Holdstein and Melissa, waiting to see, I guess, just how far Melissa would take her anger. Of the kids I liked, only Elliot was studiously bent over his work, figuring out layout. I could never be sure just how much of the real world Elliot was taking in.

"We have no objection to getting people to

1

think," Miss Holdstein said. "We just have our doubts that students are capable of thinking better than the school board."

"May I ask Mr. Malloy about this?" Melissa said. I could see how hard she was working to keep her anger under control. Her right foot was tapping to its own furious rhythm.

"Certainly," Miss Holdstein said. "Let me know what he says."

"I'll go with you," I said. The way Melissa was acting she might bite Mr. Malloy. I got my bag from under the desk and swung it over my shoulder.

"I'll go too," Elliot said, proving he knew just what was happening. I smiled at him as we flanked Melissa and left the room.

"I can't stand that woman," Melissa whispered as we walked down the corridor. "So help me, one of these days I'm going to kill her. Strangle her with her pearls."

"Don't be silly," Elliot said. "Bean her with one of those open-toed shoes."

We all giggled. Miss Holdstein's outfits were uniform regardless of weather.

"What are we fighting about anyway?" Elliot asked. "What's the issue?"

"Paul wrote this really good piece," Melissa said.

"Paul," I said. "No wonder."

"Paul wrote this really good piece," Melissa began again. "About how we should be allowed more control of our academic schedule. If there are two teachers giving the same course at the same time, we should be allowed to pick who we want."

2

"But then nobody would pick Miss Holdstein," I said.

"Nobody would pick half the teachers in this school," Elliot said. "What a good idea."

"I always figured I'd edit the *Sentinel* next year," Melissa said. "I've been working toward that since I started working on it. But I swear it's just not worth it. If being assistant editor makes me this miserable, what would I be like as editor in chief?"

"Probably a screaming, neurotic mess," Elliot said, and gave Melissa's arm an affectionate squeeze.

"What I like is the way Paul left you fighting his battles," I said. "Where is he anyway?"

"He has a tennis meet," Melissa said. "And this doesn't have anything to do with Paul. Anybody could have written this essay, and I'd be just as angry."

"We know that," Elliot said. "Don't get mad at Becca, Melissa. She's on your side."

"Of course I am," I said. "Save it for Mr. Malloy. You're going to need it there."

"Don't worry," Melissa said. "I have enough anger to go around."

We announced our presence to Mr. Malloy's secretary and waited around for a few minutes until he could see us. I hadn't had that many encounters with the principal, but what little I knew about him I disliked. That didn't mean he'd automatically side with Miss Holdstein, but it seemed like a strong possibility.

"What can I do for you?" he asked as we entered his office.

"It's a problem with the newspaper," Melissa

3

said. "We'd like to run this piece, and Miss Holdstein doesn't think we should." She handed him Paul's essay, which he skimmed.

"Nonsense," he said, handing it back to Melissa about twenty seconds later. "Of course we can't publish this."

"Why not?" Melissa asked. Her right foot was starting to tap.

"Because it isn't the function of the school paper to criticize school policy," Mr. Malloy said.

"Then what is its function?" Elliot asked.

"To report on school activities," Mr. Malloy said.

"Like drug use on school grounds?" Elliot asked.

"School activities we can all be proud of," Mr. Malloy said. "Activities which all three of you have participated in. School plays. Sporting events. Contests and awards."

"But that doesn't begin to cover what goes on here," Melissa said. "Wouldn't the school be a better place if its newspaper reflected a little more reality?"

"We don't need a rabble-rousing piece of garbage," Mr. Malloy said. "Let's present a positive image of ourselves to our readership, all right?"

What I wanted to do was punch his pompous pink face. But instead I took a deep breath and tried to sound rational. "I don't see anything negative with presenting different ideas," I said. "It seems to me that's one of the things a newspaper is supposed to do."

"In the hands of responsible journalists, certainly," Mr. Malloy said. "But I don't think anybody would really regard high school students, no matter how intelligent, as responsible journalists. That's why we have teacher advisors, and that's why you should follow what your particular advisor suggests."

"She didn't suggest," Melissa said. "She ordered."

"All the more reason to do what she says," Mr. Malloy said. "Now if that's all, I have a lot of work to do this afternoon. This may be after-school activity for you, but for me it's still part of the workday."

"Excuse us," Melissa said. She clutched Paul's essay and stormed out of the office. Eliot and I followed her.

"I want to kill," she said.

"Real sweetheart," Elliot said. "Malloy, that is. Malloy really is a real sweetheart."

"I hate being condescended to," Melissa said. "I just hate it. And that's all this school is." She scowled.

"You didn't really think you'd win this argument," I said. "There was no way Malloy was going to override Miss Holdstein."

"But it's such a good piece," she said. "And he didn't even read it. He just looked at the first paragraph and discovered there was a real idea there. A genuine unadulterated idea. No wonder he panicked."

"He didn't exactly panic," I said.

"Sure he did," Melissa said. "That sleazy little brain of his probably turned purple. He just didn't show it."

"I guess," I said.

"Whatever," Elliot said. "The big question is how to tell Miss Holdstein."

"We won't have to tell her a thing," Melissa said. "She'll know as soon as we walk in."

"That may be," Elliot said. "But there'll be some sort of ritual."

He was right. We walked back into the classroom, where the *Sentinel* staff was back at the work Melissa had interrupted. Miss Holdstein looked at us with a half smirk and said, "Well?"

"He said we can't run it," Melissa said.

The half smirk turned whole. "I guess you'll just have to grin and bear it," Miss Holdstein said.

"That does it," Melissa said. "I quit."

"What?" Miss Holdstein said. All the other kids looked up.

"I quit," Melissa said. "I've had it. This school has no idea of what a newspaper is all about. I don't see why I should waste my time. I'm crazy to stay on. I quit."

"Be my guest," Miss Holdstein said.

"I quit too," I said. "Melissa is right. The *Sentinel* is just garbage. There's a real world out there, and nobody lets us even think about covering it."

"Very well," Miss Holdstein said. "I'm sure the *Sentinel* will survive quite nicely without your contributions."

"Aw, hell," Elliot said. "I quit too."

"Then I suggest the three of you leave this room immediately," Miss Holdstein said. "And the school building, since there's no longer any call for your presence here."

"With pleasure," Melissa said. She got her bag and her books from under her desk. Elliot and I

followed her example. We looked like three out-
casts as we made our way out of the room.

"I'd kill her if she were worth it," Melissa said.

"Kill her anyway," Elliot said. "I have her for
history tomorrow."

"We all do," I said. "Do you think she'll take
this out on us in class?"

"I don't think we'll be able to tell the difference," Elliot said. "Now what?"

"Let's go to Donner's," Melissa said. "Maybe
some carbohydrates will help calm me down."

So we walked the two blocks to the diner. Occasionally one of us would snarl or curse. I didn't
do much of anything because I still wasn't sure
what I'd done or even why. Melissa was my best
friend, and I believed in loyalty, but I hadn't had
too much practice with the dramatic gesture. And
when I realized that Paul, whom I'd never liked,
was a major part of the reason I'd given up working on the newspaper, which, even if it was garbage, was fun, I got even more confused.

Sugar sounded like a good idea to me too. We
found a booth and all ordered chocolate cream
pie, a well-known cure-all.

"Hi there," Kenny said, coming over from the
other end of the diner. "What are you guys doing
here?"

"I could ask the same thing," I said, looking
around to see who Kenny had been with. He
slid in next to me, kissed me, and put his arm
around my shoulder. No matter who he'd been
with, that felt good.

"Mom's working late," he said. "I figured I'd
get a sandwich here to hold me until we had

supper. But why are you here? I thought you had a newspaper meeting."

"Newspaper?" Elliot said. "What newspaper?"

"We had a slight difference of opinion with the administration," I said. "We walked out."

"I want to kill," Melissa said. Her foot was tapping strong enough to shake the booth.

"I gather you lost," Kenny said. "Come on, Melissa, it can't be as bad as all that."

"Don't you tell me what's bad," Melissa said. "I don't know about anybody else, but I really cared about that paper. I put a lot of time and a lot of love into it, and what do I get? 'Sorry, but you're a stupid immature child and can't be trusted with any kind of decision.' Who needs it?"

"Who told you that?" Kenny asked, and I could see he was upset for Melissa's sake. I would have been jealous, but they were cousins. You could see the physical resemblance too, the sandy-brown coloring and hazel-green eyes. They were closer than many brothers and sisters. What wounded one wounded the other. I just hoped someday Kenny and I would share that sort of closeness. Melissa had been trying to get the two of us together for years, but the timing hadn't been right until last summer. Then everything fit together, and we'd been dating steadily ever since. I couldn't get over how smart Melissa had been all those years and how dumb I'd been not to listen to her sooner.

"Who told us?" she said. "Malloy, of course. And Miss Holdstein, although not in so many words."

8

"They were kind of offensive," Elliot said.

"They said we were children and fools," Melissa said. "Well, we showed them."

"No, we didn't," I said. "We walked out, but what did that accomplish? Nobody followed us."

"So what do you want?" Melissa asked. "Should we go back there and beg to be reinstated?"

"No, of course not," I said. "I'm just saying we bit off our own noses, that's all."

"My nose feels just fine," Melissa said. "I swear, Becca, sometimes I think you should write propaganda for that school."

"That's what we've all been doing for the past two years," Elliot said. "Straight party line. The school is fine, the school is perfect, there's never been any trouble at our school."

"I don't want to write propaganda," I said. "But I don't think we really proved anything by quitting."

"So what would prove something?" Melissa asked me. I could feel her anger turning on me.

"We could start our own paper," I said. "That would prove something. We could write those articles that the *Sentinel*'s never let us print. Even Paul's masterpiece. And the kind of stories and poetry that they won't let us run because they mention sex or drugs or something else we're not supposed to have heard of."

"A paper," Melissa said. "That's not a bad idea."

"Kids do it all over the place," I said. "Underground papers."

"I could really get excited by something like

9

that," Kenny said. "I hardly read the school paper because it's so boring. An underground paper that really tells what's going on sounds great."

"We wouldn't have any trouble recruiting a staff," I said. "There's the four of us, for starters, and I bet a lot of other kids would want to join."

"Paul certainly would," Melissa said.

I scowled. Everybody else laughed at me.

"We could have our first meeting this weekend," Melissa said. "Just to come up with staff and ideas."

"And a name," Elliot said. "Names are always good."

"There you are."

We looked up, and there was Richard Klein, editor in chief of the *Sentinel*. Ordinarily I liked Richard, but right then he was an intrusion.

"What brings you here?" Elliot asked.

"May I sit down?" Richard asked, and as we nodded he sat down next to Elliot. "I've been looking all over for you."

"Why?" Melissa said. "You weren't exactly a model of support back there."

"You mean I didn't duel Miss Holdstein to the death for your honor?" he said. "You're right, I didn't. But that doesn't mean I don't want the three of you back where you belong. You know perfectly well you're the three best juniors on the staff, and the paper is going to need you now and next year. So what do you say?"

"I say go to hell," Melissa said. "Did Miss Holdstein send you here?"

"Miss Holdstein couldn't care less," Richard said. "I came here on my own because the *Sen-*

tinel is important to me, and I thought to you too. Come on, how about it?"

We all looked at each other. It really wouldn't have been that hard to agree to go back. A lot of school consisted of fighting losing battles; even I, who really liked it, knew that.

So I guess it surprised everybody when I was the first to speak. "I don't think so," I said. "If we go back, there's really no point to our having left."

"Melissa?" Richard asked. "Elliot?"

"I'm tired of pretending to do real work when all I'm doing is wasting time," Melissa said. "Sorry, Richard."

"I don't dare go back," Elliot said. "These two would beat me up."

"You'll be sorry," Richard said. "Your work on the *Sentinel* was going to really help you get into good colleges. Quitting like this isn't going to look good on your records."

"Our records can stand it," I said. "Now if you'll excuse us, Richard, we have things to do here."

"Chocolate cream pie to eat," Elliot said as our waitress came back with them. Richard stared at us with disgust and, shaking his head, left. We looked at him leave and then looked at our mounds of chocolate and whipped cream and laughed.

"The thing is," Melissa said, taking a giant forkful of pie, "our paper has got to be really different from the *Sentinel*. It's got to tell the truth, even if the truth isn't that nice."

"And it's got to be honest in its fiction too," I said. "When was the last time the *Sentinel* printed a really good story?"

11

"It wouldn't hurt if it were funny too," Elliot said. "Some real humor, not the kind that Miss Holdstein thinks is funny. She thinks humor ended when the chicken crossed the road."

"Honest, well written, and funny," Kenny said. "I think we're really on to something good here."

TWO

Even I thought it was dirty.

"Does she have to look quite so much like Miss Holdstein?" I asked, holding up the cartoon. In it, a skinny woman wearing only pearls and open-toed shoes was involved in a probably impossible sexual act with a bear.

"I worked very hard on that," Lacy said. "It wasn't easy getting the eyes to cross just right."

I looked at the cartoon again. The resemblance was remarkable. It was also very funny, especially since the bear looked just like Mr. Malloy. And the caption read "Grin and bear it."

"So we're agreed?" Paul asked. "Time to print this masterpiece?"

"No point waiting," Kenny said. I looked over at him fondly. It had been fun working with him on the paper the past few weeks. It had brought us even closer together.

"Any hesitations? Any doubts? Becca?" Paul asked, and looked right at me.

"No," I said real fast. Paul didn't like me, and I knew he expected me to come up with some more quibbles. I didn't have any, and even if I had, I wouldn't have announced them just then.

My only objection had been that the picture looked so much like Miss Holdstein and Mr. Malloy that we might be sued for libel. But that seemed unlikely. Teachers weren't in the habit of suing students. Besides, Miss Holdstein ought to be flattered we even thought of her having sex. That cartoon was probably as close as she ever got.

"After we get it printed, then what?" Melissa asked.

"Then we distribute it," Paul said. "Sell the copies to the millions of eager readers, all throwing their nickels and dimes at us."

"And then it's just a matter of weeks until the Pulitzer," Elliot said. He pushed his glasses back onto the bridge of his nose and leered in cheerful Groucho Marx fashion at me.

"Do they have a Pulitzer for underground papers?" April asked. "I didn't know that."

"That's because they don't, dear," Paul said. He sounded so condescending I wanted to slug him. Still, April was his responsibility. She'd transferred to our school six weeks ago, in September, and he had made his move immediately.

I stared at all of them for a moment, one of those rare silent times when you can sit and really look. Paul was center stage, where he tended to be, holding court, making sure we all did just what he wanted us to do. April was sitting by his side, looking blond and empty-headed. She probably wasn't, but in the conversations I'd had with her I'd yet to find a brain. Kenny was sitting next to Melissa, whispering something to her.

Lacy was staring at her cartoon work. If there

14

had been recruitment for the *Southfield Shaft*, then I had recruited her. Lacy was a loner with few friends. I was one of the chosen few, ever since Lacy had discovered we both liked contemporary poetry. It made so much more sense to me than the junk they made us read in English—Longfellow and Tennyson and crap like that. Lacy liked it because she wrote poetry, and what she wrote was a lot more like what was being written now than what was written a hundred years ago. So after a few times of bumping into each other at the library, she let down her guard long enough for us to talk, and then we talked more and more, and eventually we became friends. She was so smart it scared me, with an IQ that orbited the earth, and she'd made a little world for herself with her poetry and her drawings. I respected her isolation for the most part, but I really wanted her to start dating Elliot, so I shoved her into joining the *Shaft*'s staff. Paul and the others had been reluctant at first, but when they saw her caricatures they signed her right on. She was very good.

Elliot wasn't staring at Lacy the way I'd hoped he would be. Instead he had taken out *War and Peace* and was reading it. Elliot seemed to think it was a crime to read a book with fewer than five hundred pages. I think his idea of heaven was a book, a good jazz record playing in the background, and a six-pack to nurse through an evening. Elliot had volunteered the use of a Xerox machine to print the *Shaft*. It was a gift from his hyperindulgent father a few years back. I thought about what Mr. Silvers would say if he could see what his son planned to turn out on that copier, and I giggled.

"What's so funny?" Paul asked.

"Nothing," I said. "The paper. Lacy's cartoons."

"I thought you didn't like Lacy's cartoons," Paul said.

"You shouldn't try to think," I said sweetly. "Too much stress for your brain."

"How long do you think it'll take to run off a hundred copies?" Paul asked Elliot. He was used to ignoring me.

"I don't know," Elliot said, looking up from his book. "I've hardly used the damn machine. For all I know, it doesn't work."

"It had better work," Paul said.

"It works," Kenny said. "Don't you remember, El, we tried it out when your dad first gave it to you? You wanted to print up a thousand copies of the Communist Manifesto to send to all your aunts and uncles."

"Oh, yeah," Elliot said. "It was much too long, though. I thought it was nice and short, like the Declaration of Independence."

"It works fine," Kenny said to Paul.

"And it makes good copies?" Paul asked. You'd think if he cared so much, he would have checked it out for himself.

"Professional quality," Elliot said. "Dad only buys the best."

"If I owned a Xerox machine, I'd use it all the time," April said. "I'd copy all kinds of stuff from magazines, and other people's notes and just everything."

16

"I did the first week I had it," Elliot said. "But the thrill wore off fast."

"That's you, all right," Lacy said. "Just a thrill-crazy kid."

I hoped Elliot would do his leering eyebrow thing at Lacy and offer to show her a few of his better thrills, but he just ignored her. Lacy didn't seem to mind, but I did. They were both so smart and weird. They belonged together, the way Kenny and I did.

So I walked over to Kenny and linked my arm through his. He bent over and kissed me.

"Ah, the lovebirds," Paul said. I guess he figured since we were all sitting in his family's playroom, Kenny and I should have the decency not to look so happy. I couldn't understand why, though. It was practically a documented fact that Paul scored like crazy.

"I still think a dollar a copy is a lot," Kenny said.

"We've been through this before," Paul said. "A dollar is nothing. And even if we sell all hundred copies, that's still just a hundred bucks."

"I wouldn't spend a dollar on it," Kenny said. "Besides, Elliot's father'll supply the paper. We don't have to pay for it."

"We decided on a dollar," Paul said. "It'll make bookkeeping easier. Elliot, how long will it take?"

"Hours," Elliot said. "Years. Eons. I don't know."

"It won't take too long," I said. "A day, maybe, if we all help out."

"So we can count on having copies to sell on Monday?" Paul asked.

17

"What a terrific way to spend a weekend," Elliot said.

"Definitely by Monday," I said. If Elliot and Kenny and Lacy and I worked on it together, it would be fun. Especially if Paul were nowhere near.

"I won't be here this weekend," Paul said, as though to answer my prayers. "It's my weekend for visiting Dad."

"Oh, Paul," April said. "You visited him last weekend."

"No, I didn't, honey," he said. "Last weekend I visited my grandparents."

"I never see you," she said with a pout. I wondered if she sat in front of a mirror and practiced pouting.

It obviously worked. Paul bent down and kissed her. "I'll be home next weekend," he said. "Promise."

"I'll help Elliot," I said. "And Kenny will too."

"No, I won't," Kenny said. "I'd like to, but I won't have the time."

"Why not?" I asked.

"I've been meaning to tell you," he said. "I got a weekend job at Burger Bliss. Friday nights and all day Saturday and Sunday. As a matter of fact, I'd better get going soon."

"Why didn't you tell me sooner?" I asked, breaking away from him.

"Because I'm not that happy about it myself," he said. "I'd rather be doing other stuff on my weekends."

"Then why did you take the job?" April asked.

18

"Because I need the money," Kenny said. "Becca, can you get home by yourself?"

"Yeah, I think I can handle that," I said. I was one part mad because Kenny had taken the job, and one part mad that he'd chosen to tell me in front of everybody else.

"We're still on for tomorrow night," he said to me. "Or maybe I could go over to Elliot's around seven and help out."

"No," I said. "Let's have fun tomorrow night."

"You mean running off a hundred copies of a four-page newspaper isn't fun?" Elliot asked. "Now they tell me."

"I've got to run," Kenny said. "Look, if you guys need me for anything, I'll be back of the counter. But don't expect discounts."

"At Burger Bliss you can't even expect food," Lacy said.

"Go," Melissa said with just the right amount of love and concern. I wished I had said it. I just nodded and tried to decide if I should stay mad and for how long. Was it worth it to wreck a good Saturday night? Probably not.

"Okay," Paul said after Kenny left. "Becca and Elliot will run off the copies this weekend."

"Wait a second," I said. "Isn't anybody else going to help?"

"I will," Melissa said. "I'm free on Saturday."

I had hoped Lacy would volunteer, but she was silent.

"Now, who's going to sell copies?" Paul asked. "That won't be hard. This paper will practically sell itself."

19

We were all silent.

"Come on now," Paul said. "What's the point if we don't sell a few copies?"

"Why don't you volunteer then, Paul?" I asked.

"Okay," he said. "Sure. April and I'll sell copies."

"I didn't hear April volunteering," I said.

April licked her lips nervously. "It sounds like fun," she said. "Can I do it with you, Paul?"

"You'd cover a lot more space if you do it separately," I said. "Paul in the cafeteria, and April outside maybe."

"We'll sell them together," Paul said. "I'll shill, and April'll collect the money. We'll be a great team."

"That sounds like fun," April said again. If Paul had suggested they stick their heads into an oven, April probably would have thought it sounded like fun.

"We could use more volunteers," Paul said. "How about you, Lacy?"

"Nobody'll buy them from me," Lacy said. "Nobody likes me."

"How about you, Becca?" Paul asked. "Everybody likes Becca."

"I'm going to run copies off this weekend," I said. "I've done my bit for underground newspapers."

"Elliot and Melissa will be running them off too," Paul said. "So I guess that leaves Kenny to sell. He hasn't done all that much for us anyway."

I waited to see if Melissa would jump to Kenny's defense, but she hardly seemed to be listening.

And I was still mad, so I decided not to. Besides, Paul was right. Lacy had done all the cartoons, I'd written two articles, Elliot had written a short story, Melissa had written a story and an article, and Paul had written an essay, which even I had to admit was good. April hadn't done anything, but we didn't really expect her to. Paul and Melissa had also done all the editing, and Elliot and I had done all the typing. Kenny hadn't held up his weight yet. Now that he'd have lots of good sales experience from Burger Bliss, he might as well put it to something useful.

"I guess that pretty much settles stuff," Paul said. "We should sell out by Tuesday at the absolute latest. Then we can buy some more paper, and sell a few more copies, and then we'll get together to decide what we want for the next issue."

"And then the Pulitzer," Elliot said. "Or maybe our own TV series."

"Like *60 Minutes*?" April asked. "You mean we could go investigate people?"

"He means like *Captain Kangaroo*," Lacy said. "If we're finished now, I'd like to get going."

"Sure," Paul said. "Anybody else want to stay and have a beer?"

"I would," Elliot said immediately.

"Me too," April said. "Paul's family has the best beer. It's imported from Germany."

"My stepfather has taste," Paul said. "And money."

"We know about the money, Paul," I said, gesturing at the pinball machine and the pool table.

21

I thought Paul was going to say something, but he didn't. He just shrugged his shoulders.

"I've got to go too," Melissa said. "Becca, want to walk back home with me?"

"Sure," I said. Melissa and I lived two blocks apart, and I could ask her more about Kenny's job privately. She probably knew everything there was to know about it.

"See you tomorrow, Elliot," I said as I got my jacket.

"Not too early," he said.

"After lunch," I said. "Okay?"

"Fine," he said. "See you then."

So Melissa and I left together. We ended up talking about Miss Holdstein and speculating if she ever did have sex. And I brought up the topic of Kenny's job, but Melissa didn't know any more than I did. So mostly we laughed and agreed it felt good to be outside on such a perfect autumn afternoon.

THREE

It might have been drudge work, but it was fun, too, making all those copies and stapling them together with Elliot and Melissa's help. I wished Kenny were there—a lot—and Lacy, too, for Elliot's sake, but the three of us developed our own rhythm, and we got all the copies made without too much effort.

And something about the constant movement of it, sheet into machine, copy out, hand it over, sheet into machine, copy out, hand it over, again and again, with the whirr of the machine, and the sound of the stapler, and our constant laughing conversation, made me forgive Kenny for not telling me about Burger Bliss, and then telling me when I wouldn't have a chance to respond openly. It's hard to stay angry in a whirr-and-staple environment, not when you know the person you're angry at is stuck behind a counter somewhere throwing cardboard hamburgers into plywood buns.

So by the time I got home, I was feeling perfectly fine about everything, Kenny included. The paper looked good too. Not professional, of course, but it was clean and easy to read, and the cartoons reproduced a lot better than I'd thought they would. It would give the kids at school a lot to think about and to laugh about. Worth a dollar. Maybe even two. Most of the kids at school had plenty of money, and it would be nice to be able to repay Elliot for all the paper and toner. Not that he cared.

"Have a nice day?" Mom asked me as I came in.

"Sure did," I said. "Where is everybody?"

Mom put down the paper she was grading. I couldn't remember a weekend where she hadn't brought home her students' work. "Your father is upstairs watching football," she said. "And Abby is getting ready for a date."

"A date," I said. I think it was Abby's second. "Who with?"

"Scott Samuels," Mom said. "Abby thinks he's just wonderful, but I think that's mostly because he asked her out. They have a big evening planned."

"Sounds good," I said.

"It's got to beat reading twenty-five Medieval History quizzes," she said.

"How's this year's crop?" I asked her, glancing at the test papers.

"Not bad," Mom said. "Of course college kids today do nothing but worry about their grades. Very single-minded bunch. Good grades, good job. That's all they care about."

I'd heard all this from Mom before. So I was happy when I heard Abby coming downstairs.

"How do I look?" she asked, joining us.

She looked very pretty, all dressed up in a

blue blouse and skirt. "Great," I said. "What are you and Scott going to do?"

"It's going to be wonderful," Abby said. Mom tried to look interested, but I could see her eyes straying back to the quiz. "First we're going to get hamburgers and shakes."

"Oh," I said. "If you get them at Burger Bliss, you might see Kenny there. He's working there now."

"He is?" Mom asked. "When did that start?"

"Yesterday," I said.

"I don't really approve of high school kids working weekends," Mom said. "It takes away too much from their schoolwork."

"I don't think Kenny thought he had much of a choice," I said. "His father's really slow with money, and his mother just doesn't earn that much."

"What an unholy mess," Mom said. She knew most of the gory details of Kenny's parents' divorce from Kenny's mother, who told them to everybody. "I hope it won't keep Kenny from studying."

"I don't think so," I said. "He needs good grades for a scholarship."

"After we get hamburgers, we're going to the movies," Abby broke in. "We're going to see *On the Move*."

"Hey, so are Kenny and I," I said. "Maybe we'll run into you."

"Which show?" Abby asked.

"The first," I said. "I guess we'll go out for sodas afterward."

"Mom, can I join Becca and Kenny then?" Abby asked. "Please?"

25

"Don't wheedle," Mom said. "And don't try to crash in on Becca's date."

"Scott might not want to," I said. "Don't forget, he's your date tonight."

"If he wants to, is it okay?" she asked me.

I thought about it. I wanted some time alone with Kenny, especially since it felt like I never would have any again with him. But it might be a safe bet that Scott and Abby would run into their own friends at the movie and join up with them. "Sure," I said, hoping I hadn't hesitated too long. "If after the movie you still want to. But if you don't want to, then don't think you have to."

Abby gave me a hug. "Do I look okay?"

"You asked that already," I said. "You look fine. But I'd better go upstairs and shower. Get this smell off me before Kenny comes."

"Was it hard?" I asked Kenny as we walked toward the movie theater later.

"More boring than anything else," he said. "Boring and hectic at the same time. I'd hate to work like that for the rest of my life."

"Nobody does," I said. "That's why they hire teen-agers for places like that."

"My feet hurt," he said.

"It's not that long a walk," I said. "Next year you'll have a license."

"Won't you?" he asked.

"Sure," I said. "We'll fight over who gets to drive."

"You can drive," he said. "You can do anything

26

you want tonight except eat a hamburger. I think the sight of one would make me sick."

I kissed him. "Maybe next week you'll get promoted to hot dogs," I said.

"I think I want to throw up," he said. "Do I smell greasy?"

"No more than usual," I said.

"Come on, Becca," he said. "I must have washed my hands for half an hour, but I don't feel like I got the grease smell off. Smell my hands for me, okay?"

"Sounds kinky," I said, but I lifted up one of his hands and sniffed it thoughtfully. "You smell of soap," I said. "And your hand is all rough and red."

"That's because I washed it so long," he said. "These are the cleanest greasy hands in America."

"Kenny, if you hate the job so much, do you have to keep it?" I asked.

"If I want to go to college, I'd better," he said. "I've got to save up as much money as I can. Even if I get a full scholarship, I'll still have to pay for room and board and books. Textbooks cost a fortune in college."

"Your dad'll help out," I said.

"Maybe," Kenny said. "I can't count on it, though."

"He'll come through," I said, and gave his hand a squeeze. There were some pretty rotten fathers around, and Kenny's was one of the worst, but I couldn't picture one really failing his kids. My parents were perfectly happy together, but I knew if they split up, Dad would always make sure

Abby and I had everything we needed. Kenny's father couldn't be that much different.

"You really are naive," Kenny said as though he were reading my thoughts.

"No, I'm not," I said. "I'm just naturally optimistic."

"Whatever," he said. "I hope you never change, Becca."

"I never will," I said. "Promise me you won't either."

"I promise," Kenny said. It felt wonderful walking hand in hand. I felt a little shudder of happiness. I wished Kenny weren't so tired and worried, but except for that, the moment could have existed forever and I would have been happy.

There was already a line at the movie theater when we got there. I told Kenny to get in line, and I'd go up and make sure there were tickets left. So he stood behind a middle-aged couple, and I walked up toward the ticket booth.

"Becca?"

It sounded like Abby. I turned around, expecting to see her in line with Scott. I turned around, but I couldn't spot her.

"Becca. Over here."

There are some advantages to having a name like Becca. For one, when you hear it, you know you're the one who's being called. So I kept looking, and eventually I spotted Abby. She wasn't in line at all. She was hiding in a dark corner of the movie theater parking lot.

I walked over to her. She was all alone, and I could see when I got close enough that she had been crying.

"Abby, honey, what happened?" I asked. "Are you okay?"

"He dumped me!" she cried. "I don't know where he is, and it was awful. Oh, Becca, it was so awful."

I searched in my bag for tissues and finally found a packet. I handed them over to her. Abby took them from me and blew her nose.

"Tell me just what happened," I said when it seemed Abby was in control. I looked over at Kenny, but he was still in line.

"We went for hamburgers," Abby said. "And I thought everything was going okay. Scott seemed to be having a good time. But then he said he remembered something outside, and he had to get it. I thought that was a little weird, you know, but I just said it was okay, and he left."

"And he never came back?" I asked.

Abby nodded and looked like she was about to start crying again. "I came here because I thought maybe he'd be here, but I haven't seen him," she said.

"Oh, how rotten," I said. "Look, Abby, fourteen-year-old boys can be a little weird. Sometimes they get all shy about something, and they don't know how to explain, and they just run off."

"Did that ever happen to you?" Abby asked.

"Not just like that," I said. "But almost as bad. I went to this bar mitzvah party once with some boy, and it was all his friends—I hardly knew anybody. And there were hundreds of people there, all strangers, and my date just wandered off to his friends and left me all alone for the entire afternoon. He was there, but he didn't pay any attention to me. I had to pretend to look comfortable and like I was having a good time, because otherwise one of the adults would have come over and made a big fuss over me, and then I would have died."

"What happened?" Abby asked.

"Mostly I hid in the ladies' room," I said. "And then eventually I called up Mom and Dad, and asked one of them to rescue me. Dad did, I think. It was horrible."

"Did you ever see him again?" Abby asked. "Your date."

"Sure," I said. "He was in half my classes. He didn't even apologize. As a matter of fact, he got angry at me for leaving early and not telling him when I left. I guess I should have told him, but I was just too upset."

"Boys," Abby said.

"They get better as they get older," I said. "Now what do you want to do?"

"I want to see the movie," Abby said. "Becca, I've wanted to see it all week, and this is my absolute last chance. Couldn't I see it with you and Kenny? Please?"

I looked at Abby looking up at me. Then I looked for Kenny. He was still in line, but the line was moving up.

"Sure," I said. "But we'd better get in line fast. Do you have money? Kenny and I go dutch."

"I have money," Abby said. "Oh, thank you, Becca."

"Don't be silly," I said, and gave her a quick

30

hug. "Now, let's run over to Kenny, so we can explain he's got two dates for the evening." We jogged to Kenny, swinging our arms together.

"Where were you?" he asked as we charged up toward him.

"I ran into Abby," I said. "She'd like to join us for the movie. Okay?" I tried to shoot a lot of meaning into my look at him, so he'd be filled with compassion and understanding and we wouldn't have to explain.

I guess it worked. Kenny looked at us a little funny, and then he said, "Sure, why not?" So Abby joined us. I think Kenny was a little concerned about who would be paying for Abby, because he looked relieved when she took out her own wallet and paid for herself. I would have paid for her, but I thought it would make her feel better if she did the same as Kenny and me.

We sat together, with me in the middle, and we all enjoyed the movie. After it was over, I suggested we all go out for sodas.

"If it's quick," Kenny said. "I just want to go home and go to sleep."

"No problem," I said. We walked over to the local coffee shop. It felt nice walking with Kenny and Abby, as though we were a little family. I felt close to them both.

When we sat down in the booth, I had the feeling things could get very awkward very fast. Abby was looking around, probably trying to find Scott. And Kenny really did look dead on his feet. I wasn't sure he'd be able to stay up much longer.

31

"You know, you and Kenny have something in common," I said to Abby, trying to get her attention back to our booth. "You both run."

"I didn't know you ran," Abby said to Kenny.

"I used to," Kenny said. "I don't think I ever want to run again. My feet hurt too much."

"Standing isn't good for feet," Abby said. "I don't run much, just a couple of miles a day."

"I was up to five a day," Kenny said. "But lately I've been really busy."

"It's hard with schoolwork," Abby said.

Kenny nodded. "But I miss it. I should probably just try for two miles, like you, and do it steady."

"If you ever want someone to run with, let me know," Abby said. "I used to do it with friends, but then they all dropped out, and I kept doing it, so I do it alone now. I get up really early and run before breakfast."

"That's the best time," Kenny said. "You ought to run, Becca."

"I run," I said. "I ran for class treasurer last year."

"Oh, Becca," Kenny said with a grimace.

"She won too," Abby said.

"Yeah, I know," Kenny said. "I voted for her."

"I should hope so," I said. "I ran against Mike Schwartz, and he would have been terrible."

"I think Becca should run for student council president," Abby said. "All the ninth graders would vote for her."

"Sounds good," Kenny said. "I've always wanted to be first man."

"I like politics," I said. "Maybe I'll go into it after law school."

"That would be great," Abby said. "Maybe you could be president."

"I'd settle for attorney general," I said. "Or just being a senator."

"You could do it," Kenny said. "You're one of those people who gets what she wants."

"Everyone is like that," I said. "If they really want something enough."

"Maybe," he said, but he didn't look like he believed it. By the time we'd finished our sodas, he looked as though he only wanted to be in bed, sleeping, so I told him to go home. Abby and I could manage to get back to our house by ourselves.

"Thanks," he said. "I've got to work tomorrow too."

"I know," I said, wishing he could have just half the luck I had. "Get a good night's sleep."

"You too," he said, and we parted at the coffee shop with a chaste kiss.

Mom and Dad were watching TV when we came in. I let Abby do the explaining. Then I went into the kitchen to get a piece of fruit, and Dad followed me in.

"That was nice of you," he told me as we stood by the refrigerator.

"It was no big deal," I said. "I like Abby."

"You're a good person, Becca," Dad said. And he kissed me on the forehead to make it official.

It felt good knowing he thought so.

FOUR

I was sitting in Miss Holdstein's history class on Monday afternoon, trying to pay attention and not think about her in the loving arms of a bear, when some kid walked in and handed her a note. She looked annoyed in her pinch-faced way, read the note twice, and then said, "Elliot Silvers, Becca Holtz, Lacy Kingman, and Melissa Green are all wanted in the principal's office."

We looked at each other in shock. Then Lacy got up, and we followed her lead. It felt horrible walking out of the classroom, everyone else's eyes on us. Someone snickered. Why not? He wasn't in trouble.

I tried to remember if I'd ever been summoned to the principal's office before, but the closest was once when I was in third grade. I'd been accused of playing some trick and had protested my innocence a little too loudly. So I'd been sent to the principal's office. It'd really galled me that I was innocent and being punished twice. I think I shouted that my father would defend me. I took the fact that Dad was a lawyer extremely seriously in those days.

34

"The *Shaft*," Elliot whispered as we walked down the corridor.

"We've figured that out, Elliot," Lacy whispered back.

"They can't do anything to us," I said. "Maybe a scolding, but that's all. There's freedom of the press in this country."

"I sure hope so," Elliot said.

"Let's make a run for it," Lacy said. "Now. I'm serious. Get our jackets and leave."

"Lacy, we can't," Melissa said. "Besides, it's like Becca said. Just a scolding. We were nasty little kids and we should be ashamed of ourselves. Throw a scare into us, that's all."

"I want filet mignon for my last meal," Elliot said, and he pretended a noose had been placed around his neck. He was choking when we ran into Paul.

"They got you too?" Lacy asked him.

"This is your fault," Paul said to me.

"What?" I said. Even from Paul that was ridiculous.

"You were the one who said we should have our names on the masthead," he said. "For anybody to see."

"Paul, you wanted all of us to take bylines," Melissa said. "Your name would have been there anyway. And Lacy's would have been on that awful cartoon. It's better this way."

"I thought you liked that cartoon," Lacy said.

"Look," Elliot said, "let's just wait a moment and calm down, okay?"

So we stood still.

"Our best bet is just to act cool," he said.

35

"None of us should take credit for anything. No 'I wrote this article' or 'she drew the cartoon.' We all did everything. Otherwise they'll play divide and conquer."

We thought about it for a moment, then nodded.

"And as few of us should talk as possible," he continued. "Let's be polite and quiet and let him chew us out for a while. Then we can look guilt-stricken and remorseful and Malloy will feel satisfied and we can go back to class."

"No," I said a little more loudly than I intended. "I'm not remorseful. I didn't do anything wrong, so why should I feel guilty?"

"Becca, this isn't a court of law," Elliot said. "It's school and we're students, so we're wrong by definition. Let's just go in there, get it over with fast, and save our battles for important causes. Okay?"

"Elliot's right," Paul said. "Besides, we'd better get in there before we get into more trouble. Let Elliot and me do the talking."

"Sexist," I whispered, but we all started walking again. If I closed my eyes would it turn out I was asleep and the schoolday hadn't started yet? And then I knew that even if all this were a dream, it would happen anyway. So I kept pace with everybody else and tried not to scream.

When we got to the principal's office, Kenny and April were already there, looking miserable. I thought April had been crying. I walked over to Kenny, and we linked arms, as though that would protect us from harm. Paul saw what we did and followed our lead. April looked stricken.

"Our weak link," Lacy whispered to me, and I knew she was right. Not that anybody was going to have to do any ratting. Malloy knew just what we'd done.

"Keep your mouths shut," Paul whispered to Kenny and April. "Don't say who did what, and let Elliot and me do the talking."

"Okay," Kenny whispered back. April just nodded.

"You may go in now," the principal's secretary told us, and we stood for a moment in silent panic. Then Lacy opened the door and we walked in. Having Kenny to hold on to made the walking easier.

Mr. Malloy was sitting at his desk, a copy of the *Southfield Shaft* in front of him. His face was bright red, and you could see his veins throbbing. This promised to be a scolding for the ages.

"This, I presume, is the staff of the *Shaft*?" he said as we gathered around his desk.

None of us said anything. I was glad now that I'd relinquished my spokesperson status to Paul and Elliot.

"This is monstrous," he sputtered, throwing the paper onto the desk. "Despicable. Disgusting."

April started to cry.

"I have never in my life seen such filth, such garbage," Malloy went on. "Disgraceful language, off-color jokes. I feel nauseated just sitting in the same room with you."

"So stand," Elliot muttered. Fortunately Malloy didn't hear him. I wanted to start laughing, so I

37

coughed instead. April kept sniffling. We were quite a group.

"What do you have to say for yourselves?" Malloy asked.

We kept quiet. Paul, our volunteer spokesperson, looked straight down at the floor. Elliot took off his glasses and wiped them absently.

"You should all be thoroughly ashamed of yourselves," Malloy said. "And if it wasn't bad enough writing this filth, to sell it here, on school grounds. To children. There are thirteen-year-olds here. Did you get any pleasure corrupting their innocent minds?"

I coughed again. I knew it was hysteria, but that didn't help. I wanted to laugh so much it hurt.

"Thirteen-year-olds," Malloy said again. "Innocent children. I suppose you find that funny."

I knew he was asking me, but all I could do was shake my head.

"We didn't force anybody to buy it," Elliot said. "We only sold copies to kids who wanted to read it."

"So you admit you sold it," Malloy said.

Elliot turned pale. Suddenly I didn't feel like laughing anymore.

"This cartoon," he said, pointing at Miss Holdstein and the bear. "Which one of you artists drew it?"

We kept quiet.

"Come now," Malloy said. "Surely one of you is willing to admit it. Aren't you proud of your creative work?"

38

"I drew it," Paul said coolly. "I drew everything and wrote everything."

"So did I," said Elliot. "We all did."

"Oh, a communist magazine," Malloy said. "Very convenient. Well, let me tell you, that cartoon was just one vile thing in a completely despicable magazine. I happen to be a little more interested in it because I happen to be its victim. Myself and Miss Holdstein. I don't suppose you gave any thought to what my children might think seeing such a cartoon."

From what I'd heard, that shouldn't have been a problem. Abby knew Mr. Malloy's daughter, and Malloy's family wasn't all that fond of him either.

"This will shatter poor Miss Holdstein," Mr. Malloy said. "I wouldn't be surprised if she sued all of you for slander."

I wanted to say libel but kept my mouth shut. This was no time to be cute.

"So you all did everything," Malloy said. "The slanders, the filth, the obscenities. You're all equally responsible. Even you, April?" and he whirled around to face her directly.

I held my breath. "I . . . I don't know," she whispered.

"What do you mean, you don't know?" he asked. "You must have some idea if you contributed to this filthpot."

"I . . . maybe," she said.

"Maybe?" Malloy said. "What an interesting answer. You maybe had something to do with this. And maybe you didn't. So why is your name on the masthead? Along with all these other students who did everything together?"

April just shook her head and looked down.

"You," he said, pointing at Melissa. "Did you maybe have something to do with this magazine?"

"My name is on the masthead," she whispered.

"Oh, yes, of course," he said. "But everything is unsigned. Which classic is yours? The poetry with all the four-letter words? Or the article on the inadequacy of the teaching staff at this high school? The one where you 'name names' about which teachers are best avoided, which teachers are grossly unfair in their marking, which teachers are 'professionally and personally incompetent.' Is that yours?"

"It is," Melissa said. "They all are."

"And you," he said, facing Lacy. "I suppose you wrote everything also."

"I did," she said.

"And the cougher here," he said, turning to me. "I suppose when you're not choking to death, you do your share of writing and illustrating."

"Stop picking on the girls," Elliot said. "We all did everything. All right?"

"No, it isn't all right," Mr. Malloy said. "And I wasn't picking on the girls at all. I just wanted to give them a chance to clear their names first. I was being a gentleman about it, but I don't suppose that's something anybody who would work on such a disgusting magazine would understand."

We were all quiet for a minute. Mr. Malloy looked a little less like he was about to have a stroke.

"I will not have this sort of garbage in my school," he said quietly. He was scary that way, even worse than when he was shouting. "Is that understood?"

We all nodded. I certainly wasn't about to deliver a lecture on the First Amendment.

"You rich kids," he said. "You have no understanding of how easily you can hurt people. Innocent people. Children, too. No concept, no understanding."

April started sniffling again.

"You are all now suspended from school," Mr. Malloy said.

"Hey, wait a second," Elliot said.

"If any of you is willing to admit authorship of specific articles, poems, or drawings, and write letters of apology to myself, Miss Holdstein, and to the teachers mentioned in the article about this school, you will be readmitted on Monday."

"You can't do that!" I cried. "We have rights."

"I have rights too," Mr. Malloy said. "Including the right to make your suspension indefinite, or until such time as you come to your senses. And the longer you refuse to cooperate, the worse it will be on your records. You're juniors now, and colleges will be examining those records in great detail. No matter what, there will be a black mark. But if you insist on stretching out this process because of your 'rights,' no decent colleges will accept you. If need be, I'll see to that personally."

"You can't blackball us," I gasped.

"You would be surprised what I can and will

do, Becca," Mr. Malloy said. "I suggest you don't put me to the test."

"But we didn't do anything wrong," I said. "We have rights under the Constitution."

"Your rights are what I say they are," Malloy said. "This school is not a democracy. Now I suggest you think about that for a while, while you call your parents and have them pick you up."

"My mother works," Kenny said. "She can't pick me up."

"Both my parents work," I said.

"Then have your maids pick you up," Malloy said. "You can't leave this school unless you're accompanied by a parent or parent surrogate."

"We don't have a maid," I said, shaking with anger and frustration.

"I sure don't," Kenny said.

"We have a maid," April said. "But she doesn't drive. She's from Jamaica."

"I doubt my maid would come pick me up," Elliot said. "She doesn't much like me."

"My parents are in Europe," Lacy said. "And they took the maid with them. She's never seen Europe."

"My maid ran off with Melissa's maid," Paul said. "It's the scandal of the maid circle."

"Very well, then," Mr. Malloy said. "You'll just stand here and wait until the schoolday is over. That's only two hours. It'll give you time to remember which ones of you wrote what. A chance to refresh your memories."

"My maid really doesn't know how to drive," April said.

"Then I suggest somebody teach her," Malloy said. "Not our driver's ed teacher, though, since he clearly 'plays favorites.' Someone less incompetent, perhaps."

"You don't understand," I said.

"Oh, Miss Holtz," Malloy said. "What is it I fail to understand?"

"We have constitutional rights," I said, trying to sound adult and not like a panic-stricken kid. "Rights that have nothing to do with whether we're in school or not. You can't suspend us for exercising our rights. That's just not legal."

"Perhaps it isn't legal, but I do seem to have done it," he said. "So why not make it easy on yourselves, and make it a three-day suspension. I'd hate to see you all end up in some third-rate college, or no college at all, because of some foolish 'right.' "

"My father is a lawyer," I said. "A very good lawyer. He handles cases just like this one all the time. He was the lawyer for the Birmingham Nine, and for Gerry Gitler in Chicago, and for lots of unions. He's argued cases before the Supreme Court. Cases that have to do with freedom of the press."

"I'm sure he has," Mr. Malloy said. "But this isn't about freedom of the press. This is about seven stupid students who have deliberately set out to break the rules and hurt innocent people. And I set the rules in this school. I assure you my punishment is really quite lenient. So why don't I leave you alone for a few minutes, while you try to remember who's responsible for what. Maybe

43

you'll think better in my absence." He got up, walked around his desk, brushed against Lacy without saying "excuse me," and left us alone.

"Dirty old man," Lacy muttered, and brushed herself off.

"Why didn't you keep quiet?" Paul turned on me angrily.

"Because he really is wrong," I said. "This is about freedom of the press. It is about our rights under the Constitution."

"Just because your father is some legal hotshot . . ."

"No," Kenny said. "Let Becca talk."

"If we just keep quiet and don't give in, we can win," I said. "The way it is now, he's right, there'll be a black mark against each one of us. And colleges will care. But if we take it to court, we'll win. And then they'll have to remove the records of the suspensions. It'll be like it never happened."

"We could be suspended forever, with court delays," Paul said.

"I don't think so," I said. "Look, we're out until Monday anyway. Let's at least talk to Dad, find out what our legal chances are. Okay?"

"It makes sense to me," Elliot said. "Becca's father knows what he's doing."

"If he tells us to talk and apologize and all that, then we'll do it," Melissa said. "But otherwise we should at least consider a court fight."

"Dad'll represent us," I said. "I promise you that."

FIVE

"Suspended," Dad said as we sat in the living room. "God, Becca, what got into you?"

None of this was working the way I had thought it would. For one thing, Mr. Malloy's office had called all the parents involved and told them about the suspension. So Dad and Mom knew about it before I had my chance to explain.

And they weren't taking it the way I wanted them to. Actually, they were close to hysterical. They both canceled late-afternoon appointments and came straight home. By that time Abby was home too. She'd heard most of what had happened from the school grapevine. She was on my side at least.

"Nothing got into me," I said. "I have every constitutional right to work on a newspaper."

"Don't give me constitutional rights," Dad said, and he sounded so much like Mr. Malloy I couldn't believe my ears. "You're in very serious trouble, and constitutional rights aren't going to do you a damn bit of good."

"Daddy!" I said. "Of course they will. You can take it to court. Can't you?"

45

"You expect me to act as your lawyer?" he asked. "Can you afford my fees?"

I shook my head. It had never occurred to me Dad would even suggest that we pay him.

"So why should I take your case?" he asked. "For the glory of victory? For the principle of the thing?"

"Yes," I cried. "Exactly. For the principle. We had every right to work on that newspaper."

"Did you have the right to sell it on school grounds?" he asked.

"I don't know," I said. "We hadn't thought about it."

"Becca, have you given any thought—real, serious thought—to doing what your principal—what's his name, Malone—asks?"

"Malloy," I said. "No."

"It would be so much easier if you did apologize," he said.

"Becca shouldn't have to," Abby said. "Haven't you always told us to stick up for what we know is right?"

"We're talking here about Becca's entire life," Dad said. "College, law school, beyond that. Everything that lies in Becca's future can be affected by what she decides today. All I'm asking you to do is think about the alternatives."

"Dad, if I apologize for something I don't think is wrong, then I'll really hate myself," I said, trying to think things out as I talked. "I can't help it. You and Mom brought me up to believe in things and to fight for the things I believe in.

46

You didn't see Malloy. He wasn't being rational. If he had been, we probably would have apologized, and it would all have been done with. But he was rude and abusive, and he said we didn't have any rights. He practically said he was God. I just can't see any difference between apologizing to him and apologizing to some dictator."

"Do the other kids feel this strongly?" Mom asked.

"I think so," I said. "I know some do. We don't want to just lie down and take it. We want to fight for our rights."

"Even if it could affect college?" Dad asked. "You know we've all been assuming you'd go to an Ivy League school. They might not take you after something like this."

"Then I'll go someplace else and do so brilliantly they'll let me transfer," I said. "Or I'll just plain go someplace else. Don't make me do something I don't believe in. Please."

Dad looked at Mom and then stared at the ceiling. "Kids," he said. "Why do they always believe what you tell them?"

I started breathing normally again.

"Okay," Dad said. "I want a few things understood. First of all, what you did was stupid and foolish, and you did it without any thought at all, from what I can tell. It's one thing to put out an underground paper. It's another thing to print libelous material in it. And it's quite another to sell it on school grounds. They may really have you there."

"I'm sorry," I said. "I really am."

"You should be," he said. "Your future isn't something you should toss away lightly."

It didn't seem fair that my future was in jeopardy, but obviously things had gone beyond fair.

"I don't like seeing that you've done something that could deliberately hurt a person," Dad continued. "Even if it's a teacher you don't like. They're human beings and they have feelings every bit as valid as yours. I think that's what I'm angriest about."

I wanted to cry. I swallowed hard and tried to keep looking at Dad.

"But if you weren't my daughter, I'd have to agree with you that your constitutional rights have been violated," he said. "And I think a strong court case could be made."

"Then you'll take the case?" I asked.

"Absolutely not," Dad said. "The last thing in the world I want to do is defend my daughter in court. This isn't some third-rate melodrama."

"But I told everybody you'd be our lawyer," I mumbled.

"Then you'll have to tell everybody you spoke prematurely," Dad said. "It seems to me you're caring a little too much about what everybody else will think anyway."

"Will you hire a lawyer?" I asked.

"I'll ask Jim Jordan at the office to handle it," Dad said. "He's a good young lawyer, and it'll make a nice change of pace for him. Something with a little sex to it. He should enjoy that."

48

"Don't make jokes, Phil," Mom said. "When can you get in touch with Jim?"

"Tonight," Dad said. "I'll call him at home."

"Then we ought to call all the other parents and see if they want to enter into the suit with us," Mom said. "Becca, do you have everyone's numbers?"

"I have most of them," I said. "And Paul will know April's number."

"All right," Mom said. "Your father and I will make the calls. Abby, I want you and Becca to make supper tonight. Nothing heavy, I think we're all too upset to eat very much."

"Okay, Mom," Abby said, and started for the kitchen.

"Dad," I asked as I got up, "what do you think our chances are?"

"If we're really lucky, you could be back in school by Friday," Dad said. "We'll ask for an injunction to forbid the authorities from expelling or otherwise disciplining you. We'll get the papers done tomorrow, and the judge shouldn't take more than twenty-four hours to decide."

"Friday," I said. Minimum punishment had been until Monday. The thought of Malloy having to take us in a full day before he wanted to tasted wonderful.

"That's if we're lucky," Dad said. "Never count on being lucky."

"What if we're not lucky?" I asked.

"Then we'll have to decide each step of the way," he said. "You can always apologize."

"I won't," I said. "Never."

"You'd be surprised what you'll do under the right circumstances," Dad said. "Now get us those phone numbers. Your mother and I have a lot of calls to make."

So I got my address book and wrote out the appropriate names and numbers. I knew adults believed in things like apologies and compromises, but that didn't mean I did or ever would. I believed in rights and fighting for what you believed in. Just the way Dad and Mom really did.

It took a couple of hours before Mom and Dad had gotten everyone's consent. All Dad said when he was finally through was "you owe me." And I knew I did. A lot of the parents were still so angry at their kids that they weren't willing to listen to reason, even when it was Dad who was talking. But it really made me feel better when I heard what Dad and Mom said. They were a good team. Dad gave all the legal reasons for fighting, and Mom applied all her psychological skills to convincing everyone that Dad was right and Mr. Malloy was wrong. The two of them could have convinced a brick wall to bend a little. Abby was so excited she kept talking, and I had to shush her a lot. And somewhere between Paul's excitable mother and Melissa's crying parents, we had sandwiches and salad, and didn't talk at all.

Dad called Jim Jordan after he'd gotten everybody's consent, and he let me listen on the extension as he explained what the situation was and what sorts of papers needed to be drawn up.

50

I've always planned on being a lawyer, just like Dad, and I enjoyed listening to the technical stuff, except when it hit me that the neck they were talking about was mine. Dad was also a little softer about Mr. Malloy than I thought he should have been. But Mr. Jordan obviously understood what was going on, and he and Dad mapped out strategy. They were going to use our First Amendment rights, the freedom of the press, as their main argument. And Mr. Jordan said he'd check out precedents about other underground newspapers, and students' rights to free expression in schools. It sounded like we were in good hands.

It felt really weird when everything was done that needed to be done that night. I knew I had homework to do, but I also knew I wouldn't be handing it in until Friday at the earliest. So there didn't seem to be much point in doing it. I wanted to talk to Kenny, but I didn't think it was that great an idea to call him. He'd been pretty quiet about everything, and I knew the more quiet he was, the more upset he was. I thought maybe some of my other friends would call, or someone from the *Sentinel*, but the phone didn't ring all evening.

I really didn't expect anyone from the *Sentinel* to call. If it were a halfway decent paper, there wouldn't have been any need to put out the *Shaft* in the first place.

Feeling righteous helped pass the time, and TV was pretty good too, although it was hard to

51

concentrate on it. Eventually I gave up and went to bed. The minute I went into my room, Abby knocked on my door. I let her in immediately.

"I think it's just terrible," she said, and gave me a hug.

I love Abby. Sure, we fight sometimes, but she's always with me when it really counts. And it wasn't until I felt her hugging me and saying how angry she was for me that I could start crying. I was so scared for all my brave talk. I wanted things to be the way they had been just the day before.

I think Abby was a little startled when I started sobbing, but she guided me to my bed, and we sat down together. Then she got me a box of tissues and watched me as I blew my nose, wiped my tears, and blew my nose again.

"I hate Mr. Malloy," Abby said. "I've always hated him. And his kids hate him too. You should hear what Mimi says about him."

"He shouldn't have suspended us," I said, trying to stop weeping.

"He sure shouldn't have," Abby said. "I'd like to punch him."

The image of my little sister punching out the principal made me giggle softly. Only that made me cry again. Abby just watched, and then she hugged me again.

"Abby, I was so stupid," I said. "Dad's right. I didn't think. Don't ever do anything as stupid as me, okay?"

"I won't," Abby said. "But Mr. Malloy was the stupid one."

"Did you see a copy of the paper?" I asked.

"Sure," Abby said. "A couple of the kids had copies, and they passed them around to everybody. And that article about which teachers were no good was terrific. It was all true. Except you should have put in Mrs. Engel. She's really bad."

"I didn't write that article," I said. "Paul did."

"Well, it was really good," Abby said. "I didn't have a chance to read the whole paper, but what I saw looked terrific. Something you should be proud of."

"I don't know anymore," I said. "I've never seen Dad that mad at me."

"Me neither," Abby said. "It was kind of scary."

"You should have seen Malloy," I said. "I thought he was going to have a fit."

"I wish he had," Abby said. "Was it awful?"

I nodded and gulped down some tears. "I'm so scared," I said. "What if we don't win? What if the stupid judge thinks Mr. Malloy was right? I might never get into college. I won't apologize, not ever. And then what?"

"That won't happen," Abby said. "Dad won't let it."

"He wants me to apologize," I said. "He wants me to say I'm wrong when I'm not."

"Yeah," Abby said.

"Do you think he's right?"

"No," Abby said very firmly. "I don't. I think you should fight until you win. And I know you're going to win."

"I hope so," I said. "Abby, I've just got to get into a good college. I've worked so hard."

"They'll fight over you," Abby said. "And Mr. Malloy'll get fired. Just you see."

53

"It hurts," I said. "It isn't fair."

"It won't hurt so much tomorrow," she said. "And just think how good it'll feel when you win. Will you have a party?"

"The biggest one you ever saw," I said. "You can have as many of your friends over as you want. I promise."

"I love you, Becca," Abby said, and hugged me again. We were sitting like that when Mom asked if she could come in. I said she could.

"Abby, if you don't mind, I'd like to talk to Becca alone," she said. Abby nodded and left the room. Any good feelings I might have had left with her.

Mom sat down where Abby had been, but she didn't reach out to touch me. Instead she looked away from me, toward the door.

"I'm not sure you understand just how upset your father and I are," she said, rubbing her forehead with her left hand. "Upset and angry and displeased."

"I think I know," I said.

"I don't know about the legalities," she said. "That's for your father and Jim Jordan and the courts to figure out. But it sounds like this newspaper was deliberately cruel, aimed at hurting people, and that makes us very angry."

"We weren't thinking," I said.

"No, I don't suppose you were," she said. "And you should have been. Forget the others; I didn't raise them. But I did raise you to care about something more than your rights. I raised you to care about other people's feelings, and you seem to have ignored them."

54

"Mom, teachers are mean to kids all the time," I said. "They say nasty things and they're not fair. And there isn't anything we can do."

"Except print cruel cartoons and articles," Mom said. "That's your only option?"

"I'm tired, Mom," I said. "And you aren't going to understand, no matter how hard I explain it to you."

"No, I guess not," she said. "But I want you to think about something while you're suspended from school. You know I believe in fighting battles, standing up for what you believe in. But you have to pick your battles, fight about things you really care about. I'm not sure this cruel little newspaper is worth what you might have to sacrifice for it. When you're feeling a little less defensive about things, give that some thought. It's very easy to fall into a hard fight, but to stick with it is a little harder."

"I can stick," I said, but she was already getting up, and there really wasn't anything else I had to say. So I watched her walk out, and then I got undressed for bed.

In the hours that it took before I was able to fall asleep, I did nothing but think. I just hoped that would satisfy everybody.

SIX

The forty-eight hours seemed like forty-eight years.

Dad kept me posted on all the legal developments, what specific approaches were used in the request when it got delivered to the judge, and the fact that the school decided to answer with papers of its own. I knew they would, but somehow my fantasies had been that the school board had heard about Malloy's actions and overruled him. Fired him too, while I was at it. But I guess the board decided to stick by him, the way authority figures will.

I spent those two days pacing a lot, trying to watch TV in the empty house, pretending to read. Even my hostility to Paul subsided a little; we were in this together, after all. We had a common enemy, so there was no reason to dislike each other. I had no desire to talk to anyone much, and when anyone called, I kept the conversations short. I bit my nails a lot too, something I hadn't done in four years. And I had incredible urges for junk food—potato chips, ice cream, chocolate bars. Most of the urges I gave in to, because it meant a trip to the local grocery, and that got me out of the house. They were a lonely forty-eight hours.

Of course I hadn't expected Mom to drop all her courses and stay home with me, to nurse me through my crisis. I was hardly suicidal, after all. But I wished she had offered. She ought to have known I'd turn her down, being very mature about it. But not a whisper. Hardly a whisper to me at all; she was still mad at me, and that made me mad at her. Parents were supposed to stick by their kids in moments of crisis.

Dad wasn't much better. He talked to me about the legal stuff, but as far as emotional support went, it was mostly no show. I never knew rushing into battle was such a major sin in their eyes. Or ruining one's own future. Besides, I couldn't really accept the possibility that my future was ruined. All we had to do was win, and then things would be fine again.

Tuesday evening Richard Klein, of all people, called. "I just wanted to know how things are going," he said after we'd exchanged hellos.

"Okay, I guess," I said. "I'll know better on Thursday."

"What happens then?" he asked.

"We'll hear from the judge about our injunction," I said. "If we win, we're back in school on Friday."

"That's great," he said. "Becca, one of the reasons I'm calling is because I feel a little responsible for what's happened to you."

"Good grief," I said. "Why?"

57

"I didn't exactly back you up with Miss Hold-stein that day," he said. "Maybe if I had, you wouldn't have started that underground paper."

"Don't tell me that," I said. "Melissa was the one who needed your support."

"I tried talking with her," he said. "But she wasn't willing to listen."

"She was really angry," I said. "But not at you so much."

"Well, maybe it'll all get settled soon," Richard said.

"I sure hope so."

"Uh, Becca . . ."

"Yeah, Richard?" I said.

"You don't think I'm responsible, do you?" he asked. "Even if I'd quit the paper that day, nothing would have changed. Miss Holdstein was going to make the same decision no matter what. Same with Mr. Malloy. I couldn't see any point joining you. And I did try talking to Miss Holdstein after you left."

"None of us thinks you're responsible," I said. "Not even Melissa. Malloy is responsible, and that's that."

"Thanks," he said. "I really hate the idea that I screwed up your lives."

"We knew what we were doing when we started the *Shaft*," I said, trying to sound convinced. "It had to do with the school paper, not with you."

"Great," he said. "I mean . . . well, I don't know what I mean."

"So," I said. "Is the *Sentinel* doing an article about us? 'The Shafted Seven'?"

"Of course not," Richard said. "Are you crazy?"

"Probably," I said. "What's the matter? We're not newsworthy?"

"You're the biggest thing that's happened to Southfield since the invention of finals," Richard said. "But there's no way we'd be able to get away with an article about you."

"So it's business as usual?"

"Pretty much," he said. "Except we're still understaffed. We have been since the three of you quit."

"Tough," I said.

"Yeah," Richard said. "Well, good luck, Becca. And thanks for talking to me."

"Any time," I said, and hung up with a sigh. Some things obviously never changed. I wondered if the gangland-style slaying of several faculty members at Southfield would be regarded as newsworthy by the *Sentinel*. It was almost a temptation to do it and find out. I knew right where I'd start too.

But before I went out to buy a submachine gun I decided to convey Richard's message to Melissa in person. So I went over there the next day. There was no reason not to, although it seemed decadent to be walking the streets in the middle of a schoolday. I had fantasies about truant officers nabbing me and carrying me to Mr. Malloy's office where he'd order me on the rack. With fantasies like that you can either shudder or giggle. First I shuddered; then I giggled.

When I got to her house, it took a few moments for Melissa to open the door. Her eyes were red.

"Is everything okay?" I asked her as we went into the living room.

"Yes," she said. "No, of course not. Is everything okay with you?"

"Are you crazy?" I asked. "These have been the worst couple of days of my life."

"Same here," she said. We sat down on the sofa facing the picture window. I wondered if a truant officer would wander by and, seeing us through the window, break in and seize us. I wondered if Southfield had truant officers.

"No word from the judge?" she asked.

"Do you think I'd keep it to myself if there was?"

"I'm just such a nervous wreck waiting to hear," Melissa said.

"I am too," I said. "I've bitten off half my fingernails." I showed her my hands.

"That's disgusting," she said, managing a smile. "I'm a lip-biter myself. I bite them so much they bleed."

"Yuck," I said. "What a pair we are."

"What do you think the judge will say?" she asked.

"I certainly know what I hope he'll say."

"Let me guess," she said, and we laughed together. But the laugh was strained.

"I came here for a reason," I said. "Richard called. He said he tried to talk to you, but you weren't very communicative."

"Oh, I was communicative," Melissa said. "I told him I didn't want to talk to him. I think that's communication at its most basic."

"He said for me to tell you how sorry he is about all this," I said, and gestured with my arm

60

to indicate "all this." Only it looked like I was referring to her living room. I giggled nervously. It felt odd not being comfortable with Melissa.

"He can take his sorry and stuff it," she said.

"You don't blame him, do you?" I asked. "It wasn't his fault."

"I don't know if I blame him exactly," she said. "But he's just so symbolic of what goes on. He just brownnoses and everybody smiles on him and he gets what he wants. Good grades, editor of the paper, scholarship offers. And he's nothing. No brains, no talent. It's disgusting."

I'd never heard Melissa put anybody down so. I looked at her funny, trying to think how to answer her.

I could hear the back door slamming, and then someone said, "Melissa!"

"Oh, God," she said. "It's Mom."

"What's she doing home?" I asked.

"We're in here, Mom," Melissa shouted, and sure enough, her mother walked into the living room. "What are you doing home so early?" Melissa asked.

"I have a horrible headache," Mrs. Green said. "I've had a horrible headache since the whole business began. I couldn't concentrate on work. Thank goodness my boss understands. He has a teen-age daughter too, so he knows the hell they can put you through. Hello, Becca. What are you doing here?"

"I just came to visit," I said, desperately wanting to leave.

"Of course," Mrs. Green said. "Why not? It's

61

not like you're in school anymore. You have plenty of time to kill. Your parents know you're wandering around?"

"It's okay," I mumbled.

"If you say so," she said. "So, Melissa, how have you wasted your day? I don't suppose you used the time to catch up with your schoolwork?"

"I'm not behind in my schoolwork," Melissa said.

"You will be if you don't work on it," her mother said. "If you'd worked on it, instead of this stupid newspaper, you wouldn't be in all this trouble."

"You never minded when I worked on the *Sentinel*," Melissa said. "And that took a lot more time than the *Shaft* ever did."

"Don't even mention that piece of trash in this house," her mother said. "It makes me sick just to hear its name."

"I have to go now," I sort of whispered. I didn't really want to stand up since then I'd be forced to make eye contact with Mrs. Green, but I couldn't figure out any way of leaving without standing first. So I half stood in front of the sofa. I felt really stupid.

"How do your parents feel about all this?" Mrs. Green asked me while my knees were still bent. I inched myself back to the sofa, so that it supported my legs, which I then straightened out.

"They're upset," I said. "We all are."

"I should hope so," she said. "I don't know what got into all of you, working on such garbage."

"The *Shaft* wasn't garbage," I said. "It was a good paper."

"Your parents feel that way?" she asked.

"We haven't talked about it," I said, and started walking toward the door.

"They're probably too embarrassed to talk to you about it," Mrs. Green said. "Embarrassed and ashamed."

"They are not ashamed," I said a little louder than I intended.

"If they have any sort of love for you, they're deeply ashamed."

"Oh, leave her alone, Mom," Melissa said. "Holler at me if you insist, but leave Becca out of it."

"This experience has been just wonderful for Melissa's manners," Mrs. Green said.

"I really do have to go," I said. "Melissa, I'll talk to you soon."

"Yeah," she said. "Sure." She looked cold and distant.

"Good-bye, Mrs. Green," I said, and got as far as the door before she spoke again.

"Think about it, Becca," she said as I was unlocking the door. "Think about the shame you've brought upon your parents. Give that a lot of thought, Becca."

"All right," I said, managing to escape before I threw something at her. I shook as I walked down the block. And then the nerves turned to anger. It was bad enough to get that sort of reaction from Mr. Malloy. I sure didn't need it from somebody who was supposed to be on our side. No wonder Melissa was in such a state.

When I got in, Abby was already home, lying down on the sofa, looking miserable.

"What is it?" I asked, thinking for a moment that something new and horrible must have happened.

"Oh, nothing," she said, and she moved away from me as I joined her on the sofa.

"Come on, Abby," I said. "You look awful. Was it something at school?"

"I don't want to worry you," she said. "But, Becca, they're all so mean."

"Who?" I asked.

"Everybody," she said. "Yesterday you were all heroes, but today they're just making bad jokes about you. You know what they call you?"

"No," I said. I didn't want to know either.

"They're calling you the Porn Queen," she said. "Instead of the Prom Queen. It isn't just you. They're making fun of everybody, but I feel it most when it's about you."

"Are the kids teasing you?" I asked, wanting to go back to that school and slug everybody.

"It's okay," Abby said in a voice that showed it wasn't. "I just don't see why they have to be so mean. I know they're on your side. They all liked the *Shaft*. So why do they have to make all those bad jokes?"

"I don't know," I said. "I guess they just think it's funny. But they have no business teasing you."

"I'd defend you," Abby said. "I mean I have defended you, but I don't know what to say when they just whisper and laugh. What am I supposed to do? What do you want me to do?"

"Oh, Abby," I said with a sigh. "Just try to ignore them. Tomorrow something funnier will happen, and they'll forget all about this."

I knew Abby didn't believe me, so I changed my tactics. "Tomorrow we'll win," I said. "And Friday we'll be back in school, and nobody will dare tease you then. I'll hit them if they do. No, I'll bite them. I read someplace that's even worse. Just tell me who to bite, and I'll sharpen my teeth and go to it."

Abby giggled.

"My teeth are nice and sharp already," I said. "From biting my fingernails. If you can just wait until Friday, I'll really leave my mark on Southfield."

"Oh, Becca," Abby said, laughing. "That's terrible."

"I think I'll get a little practice in on you," I said and bent down, pretending to take a big bite out of Abby's arm. Soon she was defending herself with a cushion, and we were laughing so hard we both felt almost normal again.

But as soon as I woke up on Thursday, I felt my stomach clench up like a fist. Thursday was the day of judgment. When we'd hear about our injunction. We could hear any time at all from first thing in the morning to last thing in the afternoon. I thought for sure Dad or Mom would stay home, but Mom announced she had a very important conference, kissed me in the vicinity of my cheek, and left before I had a chance to ask her to stay. Abby went off to school looking stoic; I don't think she'd smiled since our pillow fight. And Dad just said he'd let me know as soon as they heard anything, and he went off to his office.

So I was alone again, only I'd eaten all the food I'd hidden away the day before, and I couldn't go out to the grocery to get more because I had to be home when the phone rang. I couldn't call my friends, because the phone had to be free when Dad called. And I couldn't destroy any more fingernails, because they were all just memories.

So I tried screaming. Just-to-let-the-tension-out screaming, only it left me with a sore throat and not much else. Then I tried dancing. I put on a good record and started bopping and weaving, but all I wanted to do was kick the record and destroy it. I wanted to destroy a lot. I looked around the house for something to destroy that nobody would miss, but I couldn't find a single thing. So I punched a pillow for a while, but there was no satisfying crunch-and-break sound to it, so I gave that up too.

It took about two hours before I decided that what I really wanted to do was clean out my closet, so I could throw things around the room. They were a horrible two hours, in spite of the screaming and the dancing and the punching, and I probably threw out lots of stuff I'd regret not having later in life, but the rhythm of throwing things out calmed me down some. I was feeling almost normal when the phone rang, and my heart stopped dead still.

It took four rings for me to get to the phone, because after my heart stopped beating, it started pounding, and then I lost my breath, and I thought maybe I was going to die. Then I decided I wasn't about to give Malloy that satisfaction, and besides, the odds were it was good news, so I calmed down enough to pick up the phone and get out, "Hello?"

"Bad news," Dad said. He wasn't one for letting a person down easy.

I didn't say anything.

"Hello?" Dad said then. "Becca, are you there?"

So suddenly I decided Dad hadn't really said "bad news." I'd just imagined it. I was so prepared to hear it that I heard it whether he said it or not. It was just my mind playing a nasty little trick on me.

"Did you hear me?" Dad asked. "It's bad news."

"I heard you," I said, not wanting to hear what he was about to say. I knew no amount of punching or screaming was going to save me now.

"Now don't get too upset," he said. "The judge decided the case was too complex to be decided on this level. He wants to hear oral arguments before handing down a decision."

"Can you do that today?" I asked, hope welling up again.

Dad laughed. "Hardly," he said. "If the judge is real considerate, we'll be on the court calendar within a month."

"A month?" I gasped.

"Maybe less," Dad said. "But you shouldn't count on it."

"You mean I'm suspended for a month?"

"If we win, you're suspended for a month," Dad said. "Think about it, Becca. Want to apologize now?"

So I thought about it. Awful as the past couple of days had been, I still didn't want to. I was almost surprised to realize it.

"No," I said.

Dad sighed. "Okay," he said. "I'm going to set up a meeting tonight at our house with all the parents. The kids too. To decide what our next move should be."

"Shouldn't the next move be to prepare for oral arguments?" I asked.

"Yes, Becca," Dad said. "But I have to know how many of the parents will be on our side. Some of the kids might decide to apologize and be done with it. And then there have to be decisions about where you're going to go to school in the meantime. Private tutoring or what. You can't lose a full month of school. You'd never catch up."

"Do you want me to make the calls?" I asked.

"No," Dad said. "I'll make them. I want to make sure everybody has all the details straight. You can straighten up the house, go out, maybe buy some cake. Abby has a theater club meeting after school today, so you'll be alone for a while. If you want to ask one of your friends over to keep you company, do. I'll try to get home a little early, but I can't guarantee it, and I know your mother can't. Okay?"

None of it was okay. "Sure, Dad," I said.

"I'll be bringing Jim Jordan home with me, so everybody can meet him," Dad said. "He's a nice guy, you'll like him. And don't be too upset. We've lost the battle, but we certainly haven't lost the war."

"No, Dad," I said, wishing I could believe him.

"I'll see you later," he said. "Hang in there."

I would have preferred just to hang myself, but there were cake and cookies to be bought. So first I went upstairs and threw everything I hadn't sorted out back into my closet. It was an unholy mess, much worse than it had been before I decided to clean it. Seeing it look so bad made me laugh, and that made me cry, and I cried sitting on the closet floor for quite a while.

Eventually I got up and went to the bathroom and washed my face with cold water. Then I called Kenny.

"We lost," I told him, and I started getting all choked again.

"I know," he said. "Mom called me from work to tell me."

"Oh, Kenny," I wept. "We weren't supposed to lose."

"This is such a mess," he said. "You can't imagine what a mess this is."

"Kenny, could you come over?" I asked. "Please. I'm all alone here and I'm so scared and lonely."

"Yeah," he said. "There's nothing for me to do here. I've fixed everything that ever needed fixing, and I even broke a couple of things just to fix them. This apartment is in much better working order than I'll ever be."

I almost laughed, but it came out sounding like a sob. So as soon as we hung up, I washed my face again, tried to convince myself that the world hadn't ended, or that, even if it had, I had to put on a brave face for Kenny. Maybe break the toaster, so he'd have something to do while he was here.

It didn't take him long to arrive. I had one brief horrible moment when I stared down at what remained of my fingernails, and became convinced Kenny would never want to look at me again because of all the little ragged edges. I put one hand in my pocket, and opened and closed the door real fast with the other one so he wouldn't have a chance to notice.

He bent down to kiss me, and we stood that way for quite a while. That kiss reminded me just how hungry I was for a little affection. We kissed for a long time, and then Kenny broke away and said, "Damn."

"What?" I said, feeling slightly dazed.

"Everything," he said, and tossed his jacket onto the banister. He walked to the living room and I followed him, feeling slightly cheated. "You should have heard what my father said."

"You called him?" I asked.

"Mom wouldn't," Kenny said. "She blames him for this. Can you believe that? She says if he'd been around, behaving like a proper father, none of this would have happened. I need a strong authority figure, and she just isn't man enough for the job."

"What did your father say?" I asked. Kenny wasn't even sitting on the sofa. He'd taken a chair instead, so I sat down on the floor by his feet, looking for some comfort from his legs.

"Nothing nice," Kenny said, looking away from me. "Just some stuff about how he wasn't surprised I was turning out this way, given what an influence Mom was. It's amazing, how even with this mess, all they can do is blame each other."

"Oh, Kenny," I said. "I'm so sorry."

"How's your family handling it?" he asked.

"Terribly," I said. "Aren't parents awful?"

70

"Parents," Kenny said. "My sister isn't any better. Mom called her and made me talk to her. Cheryl gave me twenty minutes about how I was destroying my life and any chance I had for future happiness. How she didn't have any hope left because she didn't have a college degree and she had two young kids and was married to a bum, and what could she do? She was stuck there forever. But I was blowing all my chances with this, and if I ended up as bad as she was, it was all my fault for being so damn dumb."

"You never liked Cheryl anyway," I said. "And if you got straight A's in school and were elected class president and Yale gave you a full scholarship, your parents would still find a reason to blame each other."

"I don't know what I'm going to do, Becca. I really don't."

"You're going to fight. Maybe it'll take a little longer, but we'll win. We're bound to. And then this will all just be a bad dream, and none of us will be hurt by it. We'll all stick together, you and me and all the rest of us, and we'll get through it together. And we'll show them. Honest."

"Becca, this isn't World War Two," Kenny said. He looked at me, finally. "Malloy isn't as bad as Hitler."

"That's a matter of opinion," I said, but then I realized we could get into a fight over almost anything just then, including Adolph Hitler. So I changed the subject fast. "I saw Melissa yesterday. She seemed really unhappy."

"It's a battlefield there," he said. "Uncle Joe is

really angry at Malloy. Melissa has never been in trouble in her life, so he's sure it's the school's fault. He wanted to go kill Malloy that first night."

"That didn't seem to be the way your aunt feels," I said.

"Aunt Phyllis thinks Melissa's fallen in with a bad crowd," Kenny said. "Because of me mostly. Me and you."

"Me?"

"She thinks Melissa got involved in the *Shaft* because of you," Kenny said. "I know that's crazy, but that's how she sees it. And she's convinced we'd all be out of this with no damage if you hadn't talked back to Malloy. She thinks you're the ringleader, that you think you can get away with anything just because your father is a big shot lawyer."

"She thinks that? I'm in just as much trouble as Melissa is."

"Aunt Phyllis is feeling a little crazy," Kenny said. "She and Mom have been talking practically nonstop since this all began, and they just feed each other's crazinesses."

"Your mother doesn't blame me, does she?" I asked.

"No, she's too busy blaming Dad," Kenny said. "Don't take them seriously. This is just a bad time. They'll get over it."

"Do you think I talked back to Malloy too much?" I asked. I could barely remember what we'd said to him, I'd been so angry.

"You weren't exactly tactful, but his mind was made up before we walked in there. We could have gotten down on the floor and groveled, and he still would have done what he did."

"I hate that man," I said.

"He's not one of my favorites either."

We sat in silence for a few minutes. I tried to think what I could do to make Melissa's mother like me again. I'd known her forever, and it never occurred to me she might think I was a bad influence. It wasn't enough Malloy was costing me a month of school, maybe more, maybe any chance I had at getting into a good college. He was maybe going to cost me one of my best friends, too.

My lips started to quiver, and I bit down on them hard to keep from crying. My body shook from the effort.

Kenny looked down at me. "It's okay, Becca," he said, stroking my hair gently. "You'll get through all this."

"We all will," I said, looking up at him. "I promise."

"Yeah," Kenny said. He was still touching me, but his eyes were far away. "Maybe."

SEVEN

Promptly at eight o'clock the chaos began.

First of all, we fit an extraordinary number of people into our living room. I'd squeezed the dining room and kitchen chairs in and arranged things in a semicircle. It took awhile to sort out faces and bodies, and figure out who was there, and who was seated next to whom.

Melissa and her parents were sitting next to Kenny's mother. Kenny was half seated next to Melissa, but he didn't seem to be part of the group; his eyes were elsewhere.

Lacy and her parents were together, and they seemed to be a unit. I'd hardly spoken to Lacy since all this began. The one time I called she'd been brusque, and she seemed to have withdrawn into her shell. Mr. Silvers, Elliot's father, was sitting next to Lacy's, and Elliot was on the floor near him, looking nervous. Paul's mother had come without her husband, and Paul was standing next to her.

Mom was sitting toward the back of the room with Abby, who had insisted on being there. Dad and Jim Jordan were in the front of the living room by the fireplace. Mr. Jordan was taller than

74

Dad and was wearing one of those three-piece suits that all lawyers buy the day they pass the bar exam. I wasn't sitting anyplace. I was too busy flitting around, checking things out, offering people drinks and cake and coffee. Playing the perfect hysterical hostess.

"Is everyone here?" Dad asked once we were all as seated as we were going to get.

"April isn't here," I said. "April and her parents."

"April isn't coming," Paul said.

We all turned around to face him. "Why not?" Elliot asked.

"April decided to apologize and ask to be readmitted," Paul said. "I spoke to her this afternoon, and she told me to tell you all that."

"She can't do that!" Melissa said.

"Of course she can," Melissa's mother said. "Smart girl. You should all think about doing that."

"But April didn't write anything," I said. "Mr. Malloy said we all had to admit which articles we'd written. What's she planning to do?"

Paul licked his lips nervously. "She decided she'd say she helped me with my article on the teachers. I told her she could."

"But that was the article Malloy was angriest about," Lacy said.

"I know," Paul said. "But we had to come up with something for her to have done, and she couldn't just take someone else's work without asking permission. And she was too scared to ask anyone else."

"She could have had my cartoons," Lacy said.

"Thanks but no thanks," Paul said.

"So you just let her lie her way back into school?" I said. "And left us stuck here like this?"

"April told me she never really felt she was a part of the *Shaft* staff," Paul said. "She said she joined it because I asked her to. She said she joined it just to make friends, not because she believed in what we were doing. Her parents were very angry about the whole business. They decided to go along with the original injunction because if it worked, then things would be okay. But as soon as they found out we'd lost, they ordered April to write the letters of apology. And April didn't think it was wrong to do it."

"It is wrong," I said.

"There's nothing to be gained by blaming her," Dad said. "I'm sure there isn't a parent in this room who hasn't considered ordering his or her child to apologize. I know I certainly have."

I tried to think what I would have done if Dad had flat out ordered me. I just couldn't picture him doing it.

"Then I gather there are six students who are suing," Jim Jordan said. "Six from the original seven."

"That's right," Elliot's father said. The other parents buzzed and nodded in agreement.

Mr. Jordan stood up straight and tall. "My name is Jim Jordan, and Mr. Holtz has asked me to represent you," he said. "I wrote the papers for the injunction request. I'm here to discuss legal strategy and explain whatever I can to you. First of all, just because we didn't get the injunction no one should think we're going to lose the case.

76

Judge Denning simply felt the issues were too complex to rule on without a hearing."

"Do you know what issues in particular?" Melissa's father asked.

"My guess would be that the newspaper was sold on school grounds," Mr. Jordan said. "That seems to be their strongest point."

"Do we have an answer to it?"

"I can think of several," Mr. Jordan said. "Things certainly would have been easier if the paper had been sold exclusively off campus. But we're stuck with the fact that it wasn't."

I tried to remember whose bright idea it was to sell the newspaper at school, but it didn't seem like we'd even thought about it. We just assumed that was the best place to sell it.

"I haven't completely worked out the trial strategy yet," Mr. Jordan said. "And I'll be eager to have individual conferences with all the students and their parents to discuss things when they're more developed. Right now I just want to reassure you that we do have a strong case, and I'm optimistic that we will win, and that it won't take a long time."

"How much time do you think it will take?" Lacy's mother asked.

"The judge understands the need for speed," Mr. Jordan said. "The case will probably be heard before Thanksgiving."

"Thanksgiving," Melissa's mother said. "But that's a full month away. What are the kids supposed to do in the meantime?"

"I have a few words to say about that," Elliot's

77

father said. "I happen to have some very good friends on the board of trustees of the Merwin School. I called them this afternoon and explained Elliot's predicament to them. They were naturally sympathetic."

"Naturally," someone muttered. I couldn't be sure but I thought it was Mom.

"They have agreed to take all seven—well, I guess it's six now—students on a semester-to-semester basis," Mr. Silvers continued. "In other words, if you pay a full semester's tuition, you can have your child there until the end of this semester. If you choose, you can then take your child out, or pay the next semester's tuition and your child can stay for the full school year. I must say I thought this was quite generous of them and, given the circumstances, I think it's a good working solution."

Kenny's mother pressed her lips. I knew they didn't have that kind of money. Kenny just stared straight ahead.

"If we win, we won't have to stay there, will we?" Melissa asked.

"No, of course not," Mr. Silvers said. "That would be each family's choice."

"How much is a semester's tuition?" Paul's mother asked.

"Twelve hundred," Mr. Silvers said.

"Do we have to decide immediately?" she asked. "My husband isn't here."

"You all have the weekend to decide. But I've decided that Elliot will be attending. I don't think he can afford to lose an entire month's schoolwork. Or, should we lose, even more than that."

"What's wrong with the kids' apologizing?" Melissa's mother asked. "This could cost us all a fortune. Twelve hundred for tuition, and heaven knows what the legal fees are going to be."

"I'm volunteering my services," Mr. Jordan said. "There will be court costs, of course, but they shouldn't be too high."

"Even so," Melissa's mother said. "What would it cost for each kid to admit what he or she's done and write a little letter of apology? Mr. Malloy was right. It was a dirty, filthy newspaper, and I'm ashamed that my daughter had anything to do with it."

"Mom—" Melissa began.

"You heard what Phil Holtz said," she told her. "He practically ordered Becca to apologize. I think it's crazy that none of us have the common sense to make our kids apologize and save us all money and heartbreak and heaven knows what else."

"Mom, I'm not going to apologize," Melissa said. "You can order me to to your heart's content, and I still won't do it. You can write a letter for me to sign and I won't sign it, and if you forge my signature I'll just deny I signed it, and if the school decides to forgive me on those terms I'll refuse to go back."

"You're tossing away your entire future for a piece of garbage," Melissa's mother said. "For some worthless friends. For some constitutional principle you don't even claim to understand. We raised a bunch of spoiled brats, and none of us has the courage to stand up to our own children. My mother would have whacked me good if I'd ever done anything like this."

"I stand one hundred percent behind my son," Elliot's father said. "And I'm sure the other parents in this room do too. If you're so worried about the legal fees, I'll pay them. Does that reassure you, Mrs. Green?"

"I think we're all a bit tense here," Mom said from the back of the room. "I certainly understand how Phyllis feels. But we've raised our kids to believe in themselves and in standing up for their rights. And their rights have been violated."

"That certainly is obvious," Mr. Jordan said. "From birth until death, every American citizen has the right to freedom of the press. And that's exactly what the high school is trying to deny these six kids."

"Can you guarantee that we'll win?" Melissa's mother asked.

"No one can guarantee anything about the legal system," Dad said. "But Jim and I are going to present the strongest possible case, and I'm confident."

"On this level?" Lacy's father asked. "That's something to be considered too, you know. How many appeals it's going to take."

"Judge Denning has a good record on this sort of thing," Mr. Jordon said. "He's a liberal, fair-minded man. We're lucky that he's hearing our case."

"If this has to go all the way to the Supreme Court, Melissa will be thirty years old by then," her mother said.

"Of course if we lose on this level, we'll all have to reexamine our options," Dad said. "But we seem to have the upper hand, since we can always choose to obey Mr. Malloy's request and hand in apologies."

"I won't apologize," I broke in. "I don't care how many years it takes."

Dad ignored me. "Are there any other questions?" he asked.

"I want to know more about this Merwin School," Paul's mother said. "To tell my husband."

"You know the school, Mom," Paul said. "It's the one on the hill past the shopping center."

"I know where it's located," she said. "But what sort of school is it?"

"The Merwin School is a private school, kindergarten through high school," Mr. Silvers said. "The classes are very small; they ordinarily keep their grade size to fifty kids total. That's one reason why it's so nice of them to agree to take in our seven. Six. It's a progressive school devoted to encouraging children to use their own minds and be resourceful."

"It seems to me that's just how our kids got into trouble in the first place," Melissa's mother said.

"If it's such a good school, why didn't you send Elliot there?" Paul's mother asked.

"Mom!" Paul said. I'd never seen him look embarrassed before.

"Elliot's mother had been a schoolteacher before she died," Mr. Silvers said. "And she always believed in the principle of public education. Naturally, after she died, I decided to follow her wishes on this matter and kept Elliot in the local school system."

I tried not to look at Elliot. His mother had

81

died four years before in a car accident. He didn't mention her much, and I always tried to remember not to around him.

"The Merwin School has an excellent reputation," Mom said. "Phil and I considered it for our daughters when we first moved here. Since the public school system is excellent, we couldn't see any need for a private-school education. Then."

"Do their kids get into good colleges?" Paul's mother asked. "That's so important."

"It's a college prep school," Mr. Silvers said. "And many of their students attend Ivy League schools."

I tried to remember the kids I knew from Merwin, but I'd only met a couple of them, and that at parties. The Merwin kids didn't mix with the kids from our school.

"The alternative would be individual tutoring?" Lacy's father asked.

"Or no tutoring at all," Mr. Silvers said.

"Or getting our kids to come to their senses," Mrs. Green said.

"Mom," Melissa said. "Can we just drop that?"

"This is all so unfair," Kenny's mother said.

We were all silent for a moment. That was the first thing she'd said all evening. Kenny had just barely said hello to me. I'd almost forgotten they were there.

"I know the kids are right," she said. "I really do know that, although I certainly wish Kenny and Melissa, and the others, hadn't gotten involved in such a . . . such a thing. But I believe in freedom of the press, and really it is all so harmless. They didn't rob a bank, after all, or sell drugs, or anything violent or illegal even. Just work on a newspaper. Really, they're all good kids."

"Hear, hear," Mr. Silvers said.

"But it's so much money," Kenny's mother continued, ignoring him. "And so much worry. So many problems. I know none of this is easy for any of you, but at least you have money. Since the divorce, well, money's been scarce."

This time it was Kenny who muttered, "Mom."

"Kenny says I talk too much about the divorce," Kenny's mother said. "Maybe I do. But that's not the point. The point is it's just all so unfair. Why our kids? Why were they singled out when there's so much worse going on? Drugs. Drinking. Shoplifting. I read the papers. I know what's going on. Why our kids?"

"Malloy doesn't like us because we think," Paul said. "We stand up for what we believe in, and we aren't ashamed to disagree with him in public."

It wasn't that I disagreed with what Paul said, but I just wasn't in the mood to hear him say it. Paul would turn his own funeral into an opportunity to make a speech. So I inched my way into the kitchen as inconspicuously as I could.

Elliot must have noticed me, since he came in right afterward. "I need something to drink," he said.

"The soda is in the refrigerator," I told him.

"You have anything stronger?" he asked. "I don't think I can take much more of this sober."

"Paul will drive me to drink too," I said. "I think there's still some beer in there."

83

Elliot looked around the refrigerator and found a bottle. He opened it and chugalugged it.

"This has brought out the crazy in Dad," he told me. "He hasn't gone to work in the past three days. He just stares at me and worries."

"I wouldn't mind if my parents had acted like that," I said. "They seem to feel I should be handling all this on my own."

"Let's trade then," he said. "One smothering father for two neglectful parents. That sounds like a reasonable deal."

"Throw in a utility infielder and I might consider it," I said.

"It isn't like Dad is blaming me," Elliot said. "I think I could take that better. He's just trying so damn hard to make things better for me."

"It sounds like heaven," I said. "Forget the infielder."

"You know what he threatened to do today?" Elliot asked. "When he found out about Merwin? He offered to stay home from work tomorrow and go shopping with me. Buy a whole new wardrobe for Merwin. Something preppy."

"Your father likes to spend money on you," I said. "You know that."

"I know," Elliot said. "But a new wardrobe? Jeez."

"You don't think we'll really need one?" I asked. "They must dress pretty much the same as we do."

Elliot laughed. "Don't worry, Becca," he said. "You'll knock 'em dead no matter what you wear."

"Wear to what?" Lacy asked, coming into the

kitchen. "Is this a private wake or can anyone come in?"

"No speeches allowed," I said. "Otherwise all are welcome."

"Paul is still at it," Lacy said. "Poor Mr. Jordan is staring at him with his mouth wide open."

"Paul certainly is an experience," I said. "We're talking about what to wear to Merwin."

"Merwin," Lacy said. "I know some kids who go there, and it sounds better than Southfield. But I'll have to see it to believe it."

"I don't care how great Merwin is," I said. "Southfield is where I belong."

"You're such a sentimental fool," Lacy said. "Becca, no matter what happens, it won't be the same. Even if the trial were tomorrow and we won right smack there and were back in on Monday, it would all be different for you."

"Not for you?" I asked.

"I never fit in at Southfield," she said. "Nothing would change that. But you were the golden girl. Great grades. School offices. I'm surprised you aren't a cheerleader."

I blushed. I'd thought about trying out for cheerleading, but my schedule had been too crowded.

"It's never going to be the same for you," Lacy said. "You've got a blot on your perfection."

"Come on, Lacy," Elliot said. "You don't have to be mean."

"I'm being honest," Lacy said. "I'm just marking time until I graduate. I think you are too, although not as desperately as I am. But Becca, and Paul,

85

too, and Melissa, and even Kenny, all love where they are. What they are. And they won't ever be that again."

"If we win the case, the suspension will be erased from our records," I said, but I knew it sounded hollow.

"Oh, Becca," Lacy said. "I really am sorry for you." She patted me on the head and walked out.

"I think I'm going to scream," I said.

Elliot looked at me and laughed. "If it's any comfort, Becca," he said, "I'm a lot sorrier for me than I ever will be for you."

I shook my head. "The ones we should be sorry for are the people who've been listening to Paul," I said, trying to laugh. "Want to go back in and rescue them?"

"Not especially," Elliot said, but he followed me out of the kitchen. Paul and Melissa's mother seemed to be having it out, with Dad who was trying to get things back to normal. I gazed at everybody in the room and wondered miserably when I would start liking my life again.

EIGHT

Saturday evening we all bustled so you would have thought we were a normal American family. Dad and Mom had both been deliberately busy since Thursday night's meeting, and they'd spent most of Saturday working. Mom was preparing midterms and Dad worked on a brief. Neither one worked at home. It wasn't unusual for them to be working on a weekend, but usually one of them managed to make do at the house. For both of them to be out struck me as a little obvious.

But they both got in Saturday afternoon in time to prepare for a dinner party they'd been invited to before all the troubles began. They acted like things were normal, so I pretended to also, discussing with Mom the questions she'd come up with and with Dad the details of his case.

Abby had decided to give dating a second chance and was preparing to go out with Larry Simon, fifteen years old and *very* sophisticated, according to her. I listened to endless discussions about which sweater she should wear and giggling reports about Larry's good looks.

I didn't have a chance to see Larry because, by the time he came, I was upstairs washing my own hair and debating what I should wear for my date with Kenny. I'd called him the night before, and although he'd sounded harried he'd said he would try to see me Saturday night. I decided he probably wouldn't see me, and spent Saturday afternoon wasting time, going over my clothes, trying to figure out what I should wear to Merwin. It wasn't until I saw everybody else preparing to go out that I decided I looked like a royal mess and should start getting ready, just in case Kenny made an appearance. So I missed Larry Simon, but I did have a chance to say good night to Dad and Mom before they left for their dinner.

The house had been empty all day, but it seemed emptier somehow now that it was nighttime. I suddenly wished I hadn't wasted the entire day worrying about my wardrobe, and had done something intensely physical instead. Swimming the English Channel sounded appealing, or digging a ditch. I wanted my body to ache from tiredness rather than nerves.

It was a little late, though, to start something, especially since I didn't want Kenny to find me hot and sweaty. Not after I'd already showered and washed my hair.

Not knowing what else to do, I sat and tried to read. It was hard to concentrate, however, and eventually I gave up and turned on the TV. There was nothing on I really wanted to watch, so I tried to combine the noise from the set with reading, but that only made things worse. I kept the set on but turned the sound off, and tried to keep reading. It wasn't long before I started getting a headache.

That was when I started staring at the clock, which was what I wanted to do anyway. It was 8:42 and if Kenny got there by 8:50 we'd still have time to make it to the movies for the 9:30 showing. After that the line would probably be too long. The second hand swept around the clock until it was 8:48. Just as I was getting ready to stop watching and start screaming, the doorbell rang.

I ran to the door, and sure enough there was Kenny. I opened it and said, "I'll get my coat."

"Coat?" he asked. "Can't I come in?"

"I thought we'd go to the movies," I said.

"Oh, Becca, not tonight," he said. "I'd collapse. Some other time, okay?"

"Sure. Come on in."

He followed me into the living room and tossed his jacket on the banister. "I'm exhausted," he said with a sigh.

"Sit down," I said, pointing to the sofa. He sprawled on it, leaving me just enough room to get next to him. "Want something to drink?"

"No, thanks," he said, and patted the couch. So I climbed in, and he slipped his arm around my shoulder. For a big sofa, things were quite cozy.

We kissed, and that felt better than anything had in a long time. I didn't want to break away and neither did Kenny, so we clung together, giving each other the support we both needed. The sofa became a little world all its own.

"Oh, Becca," he sighed. "I love you, you know that."

"I love you too," I said, and before I had a chance to say anything else we were kissing again, our hands stroking each other, gently at first and then with increasing passion.

"Make love with me, Becca," he murmured. "Please, Becca, tonight."

I don't think I ever wanted to do something that much in my life. I kissed Kenny deeply and tried to think at the same time. It wasn't easy.

"We're alone," he whispered. "Please, Becca."

"I can't," I said, breaking away from him. "Kenny, stop."

"What are you talking about?" he asked. "Come on, Becca, what's the problem?" He started rubbing my back, which didn't make being rational any easier.

"Not tonight," I said. "Tonight I'm jinxed."

"What are you talking about?" he asked, kissing me on my neck. I grew increasingly aware that the only part of my body that wasn't a hundred percent enthusiastic was a mean-spirited section of my brain.

"It wouldn't work," I said, trying to sound rational. It wasn't easy to be rational with Kenny kissing my neck. His hands found my breasts, and that certainly didn't cool things off.

"Stop!" I yelped. I sounded like a puppy.

Kenny stopped, though, so I guess it worked. "You know you want to," he said. "Come on, Becca."

Desperate times called for desperate measures. I sat up straight. My body was quivering, and I think Kenny sensed how torn I was because he bent his arm at the elbow and rested his head on his hand to have a better look at me. I tried to look at him sideways, but he just seemed amused, almost smug. My body quivered a little less.

"Not tonight," I said. "Not the way things are going."

"Things are going just fine," Kenny said. "Things are going better right now than they've gone for either of us in a long time."

"Now sure," I said, taking a deep breath. Kenny's free hand had made its way to my back and was rubbing it gently. I tried shifting my weight so my back wouldn't be quite so accessible.

"Abby will be home soon," I said.

"We'll go to your bedroom," he said. "She won't know a thing."

"My parents," I said. "The dinner party will be called off, and they'll come home early."

"When did they leave?" Kenny asked. He'd shifted his body slightly, and his hand was back by my right shoulder, massaging it.

"An hour ago," I said. "More."

I didn't mean more massage, but Kenny decided that was what I'd meant, and soon both hands were giving my back a sensual rubdown.

"No," I said, wiggling my back. "I mean they left more than an hour ago."

Kenny laughed. "You know, you're crazy," he said, and he was back at my neck. For one mindless golden moment I gave thanks that I'd showered and refrained from physical effort.

But then the mind kicked up again. "Kenny, I said stop it!" I half shouted. "I don't want to. Not tonight."

"Don't lie, Becca," he said. "You know you want to. You want to as much as I do."

91

"I'll get pregnant," I said. "Things are not working for me these days, Kenny."

"I have protection," he murmured. "Honest."

"Triplets," I said.

"What?"

"I'd have triplets anyway," I said. "I told you my life is jinxed right now. One good time and I'd be stuck with triplets."

He laughed long enough to stop stroking me. I used the break in the action to sit up again and straighten my clothes. I felt like Miss Holdstein, all prim and proper.

"You wouldn't have triplets," Kenny said, but he started straightening himself up too. Soon we were just sitting on the sofa, his arm around my shoulder. I felt very dumb, but I knew better than to ask him just how he felt. Some answers you don't want to hear.

"So," I said, trying to sound normal. "Did you have a nice day today?"

"I had a crappy day today," Kenny said. "I put in eight hours at Burger Bliss, and then I came home to a hysterical mother. Why? How was your day?"

"Not as bad as yours," I said, licking my lips nervously. We sat there feeling strained and uncomfortable for a few moments, until I could think of an excuse to say something different. "Are you thirsty now?" I asked. "Or hungry? I could get you something."

"Soda sounds good," Kenny said, so I sprang up from the sofa and scurried to the kitchen. I took a while deciding which can to open and which glass to use and whether to pour it myself and leave the can behind or to bring Kenny the can and the glass and let him decide for himself. It seemed like a very important decision to make.

I must have taken longer than I realized because Kenny came into the kitchen. "What's going on?" he asked. "Do you have to harvest the soda?"

"No," I said, handing him the glass and the can. "Do you want ice?"

"No," he said. "I got enough of that from you."

I scowled.

"Becca," he said, and he took my hand. He held it gently for a moment, and then let it free. "I do love you," he said. "That's all. I didn't just say it. I meant it."

"I know," I said. "I'm sorry, Kenny. I just feel so disaster prone."

"I know the feeling," he said. He took a sip of the soda, and then put it down on the kitchen table. "I can't believe I asked for this," he said. "I served this stuff all day long, and I swore never to look at another glass of it again."

"Would you like something else?" I asked. "Juice? Milk?"

"No," he said. "Do you love me, Becca? Really?"

"I really love you," I said. "Why?"

Kenny smiled. "Does there have to be a reason?"

"I'm not going to go to bed with you," I said. "Not tonight. No matter how much we love each other."

"I just wanted to hear you say you loved me," he said. "That's all. That was my reason. Right now I need you to love me. I'd love to go to bed with you, but I need your love more. Understand?"

I didn't completely, but I nodded anyway.

"I'm glad you love me," he said. "It makes things easier."

"What things?" I asked, wanting to hold him and knowing just what would happen if I did.

"Everything," he said, shrugging his shoulders. "Life. Breathing. Will you love me always, Becca?"

I wanted to say yes, so I did. But it didn't sound real to me, so I added, "Probably."

"Probably," Kenny repeated. "You're no Juliet."

"Juliet had fingernails."

"Is that it? I love you without fingernails."

"Oh, Kenny," I said, and hugged him. "I do love you, Kenny. I really do. Please believe me."

"I know," he said. "I believe you. And I understand."

It felt comforting being in his arms again, but I still didn't want to be the mother of triplets, so I broke away as gently as I could. "Want to do something?" I asked. "Watch TV maybe?"

"Yeah, sure," he said. "That sounds good."

So we walked back to the living room hand in hand. I turned on the set and we found something we didn't have to pay too much attention to. I sat upright on the sofa, and Kenny rested his head in my lap. I stroked his hair gently and tried to figure out why one character on the show was convinced another was out to kill her.

Within a few minutes I could hear Kenny breathing slowly and deeply. I looked down, and sure enough he'd fallen asleep. At first I was offended, but then I just felt sorry for him. I sat there, half watching TV, half thinking about how confusing everything was, feeling the weight of his head on my lap until eleven o'clock when I kissed him on his forehead.

"Don't worry, Kenny," I whispered into his sleeping ear. "Everything will work out fine. I promise."

I lifted his hand to my lips and kissed it, then shook him gently to wake him up. He was startled at first, but then he realized what had happened and apologized.

I smiled at him, and we walked together to the front hallway where he put on his jacket. We kissed good night and then I watched him leave by the light of the TV set.

NINE

"Ready for school?" Dad asked me Monday morning. He was sipping his coffee as I came into the kitchen.

"As ready as I'll ever be," I said. I was dressed in something I trusted was appropriately preppy, not at all sure that was the right approach. Artsy might have been a better choice. Or sackcloth and ashes.

"I can't really say I'm happy about all this," Dad said, carrying his mug to the sink and rinsing it out. "But it should be an interesting experience."

"I suppose," I said, pouring myself some milk. "Can you give me a lift this morning?"

"Your mother will," Dad said. "She has more free time this morning. As a matter of fact, I'd better get going. Can't count on the train to be late."

I watched as he put on his jacket, gathered his briefcase and his coat, and made his way outside. I wanted to go with him, the way I had when I was a little kid and he'd take me to see where he worked. No train ride for me today. Instead I finished the milk and rinsed out the glass.

"Ready to go?" Mom asked me, peeking into the kitchen.

"As ready as I'll ever be," I said.

"Fine," she said, and cut through the kitchen to get to the back door. I followed her out silently.

The Merwin School was set off the road, hidden by acres of lawns and trees. I'd driven past it many times, but I'd never really looked at it. There had never been a need to before.

"It'll be all right," Mom told me as we drove into the parking lot. "And if it isn't, you do have options."

"It's only for a month," I pointed out, glad we were finally talking about it. "Maybe even less."

"Will you be able to make it home all right?" Mom asked as she parked the car. I stared nervously at the back of the school building.

"Sure," I said. "Maybe I'll walk home with Melissa. Or Elliot's maid might give me a lift back. I'll manage."

"Make the best of it," Mom said. "See what you can learn."

"Okay," I said. My hand reached for the door handle, but I didn't open the door. I wanted her to hug me, to say it would all be over with soon, to say I was right, and that she respected my stand and didn't begrudge me the battle or the pain or the money. The money I knew was the least of it, but it was there, along with the unspoken anger. And the spoken anger for that matter. The hug, kiss, or little loving gesture wasn't there.

"I'll see you tonight," Mom said, and I said "yeah" and opened the car door.

97

Mom's hand brushed briefly against mine. "It'll be okay," she said. I nodded and got out.

I found Elliot in the back of the building, and the two of us walked together to the main office. "I want a drink," he said.

"It isn't even nine," I said.

"I don't care," he said. "I need one."

"Hold out until lunch," I said. "Maybe they have a soda machine."

"Becca, you don't understand," he said, and I looked at him and realized he was right. I didn't understand. He was standing there, pale and shaking, and this time when he said, "If I don't have a drink, I'm going to go crazy," I believed him.

So I hugged him. I gave him the hug I'd wanted so much all day. One of us might as well have it. "Come on," I said. "You can make it. I need you to make it."

"I really don't feel good," he mumbled.

"Welcome to the club," Paul said. I hadn't seen him walk up, but there he was, and for once I was glad. "Come on, Elliot, let's show them our stuff."

I snickered.

"Okay, then," Paul said. "Let's fake it. Let's act like this is all nothing. Let's try to fool somebody, at least."

"You two go in without me," Elliot said. "I just need some time outside. I'll be okay."

I was casting desperate looks at Paul when Lacy approached us. "Let's get this turkey on the road," she said, and opened the door.

"Ah," Elliot muttered. "Miss Congeniality."

That did it. I just roared with laughter. Soon Paul and Elliot joined in.

"We've got to get in there," Paul said. "Before they suspend us for tardiness."

"Have either of you seen Kenny or Melissa?" I asked.

They shook their heads. "Maybe they're inside already," Paul said.

"I guess," I said. "I tried to talk to Melissa this weekend, but she wouldn't come to the phone."

"What about Kenny?" Paul asked.

"He should be here," I said. "But you know Kenny. He tends to be late."

"Anyone hear from April?" Elliot asked.

"I did," Paul said.

"You're not still dating her?" I asked.

"I don't know," Paul said. "Maybe."

"Paul!"

"This isn't the time or the place," Paul said. "Come on. We're late already."

I knew he was right, but, as much as I wanted to slug him, I just followed him into the school building. I held Elliot's hand and half guided him in.

We found the administration office, where we were told to report to our new homerooms. Paul, Elliot, and Lacy had been assigned to one, and me to another. After I parted company with them, I made my way alone to Room 4A. I half prayed I'd find Kenny and Melissa in 4A, waiting for me.

But there were no familiar faces when I got there. Just a teacher and about twenty kids, seated in little clusters of desks. It didn't even look like a proper classroom. The desks weren't aligned, and suddenly I knew I wouldn't even have the convenient crutch of alphabetical order. There would just be these twenty-odd kids, who'd known each other since kindergarten, moving and shifting about with ease, while I stared at them, and tried to commit faces and names to memory, and would never be sure who was who, let alone why and how and where and what. Did any of them have any idea how frightening they could be en masse? I wondered what sort of first impression it would make if I fainted.

But I didn't faint. I walked up to the teacher and said, "My name is Becca Holtz, and I'm one of the kids from Southfield High."

"Of course," the teacher said. "We've been expecting you."

I swallowed hard.

"There's an empty desk in that cluster over there," the teacher said. "Why don't you take it for today?"

"Are there assigned seats?" I asked.

"Oh, no," she said. "We don't believe in that sort of artificial structuring here."

"Oh," I said. Terrific. Every day there could be a different alignment of faces and names. No structure whatsoever. A whole new set of rules. Possibly better rules than the set I'd left behind. Possibly rules I would have loved back at Southfield. But rules I really hated here.

"My name is Nancy Shorter," the teacher said, holding her hand out for me to shake. I took it, almost not knowing what to do with it. Then I remembered, and I shook it, trying to smile. I couldn't remember if I'd ever shaken an adult's hand before. My own hand suddenly felt very sweaty.

"I'm sure you'll get the hang of this before too long, Becca," she said. As I started making my way to my new temporary headquarters, she said, "Kids, this is Becca Holtz. Try to make her feel at home."

"Get out the hash," someone said.

"Not *that* at home," the teacher said. I'd already forgotten her name. Some politician I'd make.

"Hey, Nancy, when is that team project due in?" another kid asked.

"Thursday," the teacher replied. They called the teacher by her first name! I tried to picture calling Miss Holdstein Irma, but the image was just too much for me.

A bell rang, and I nearly jumped with relief. At least they still had bells. Any structure in a storm.

Sure enough, some of the kids got up and started moving around to other rooms. I walked back to Nancy and showed her what I assumed was my schedule.

"You stay here for the next mod," she said. "Then your next two mods are up to you, but you might just like to wander around and see what's going on."

"How long is a mod?" I asked.

"A half hour," she replied as other kids started coming in. Thank goodness, Elliot and Lacy were

101

in the crowd. Elliot and I immediately took seats next to each other, but Lacy sat down next to the girl she'd been talking to when she walked in.

It turned out the class was plain old English. Well, maybe not as plain and old as the English I was used to at Southfield, but at least there was a family resemblance. Instead of studying Shakespeare, we concentrated on the later plays of Edward Albee. Most of the mod was devoted to a critique of his newest play, which a few of the kids had seen over the weekend. Nancy spoke freely in the discussion, and nobody raised hands. It was an intellectual free-for-all. Even if I'd had an opinion, I would have been too scared to offer it.

I can't say I missed Tennyson and Longfellow, but a textbook would have been comforting. None of the kids seemed to have one for English. Just notebooks and paperbacks.

Somewhere in the distance, that blessed bell chimed again. Everybody got up, jostling about. I wanted to join Lacy, but she was talking with a couple of other kids, so I left with Elliot.

"Where do you go to next?" he asked.

"I don't know," I said. "I don't think I have to be anyplace."

"I'm due at gym," he said. "Can you imagine? They still have gym."

"Gym," I said. That was my second-period class at Southfield. Volleyball. I wondered if they volleyballed at Merwin.

"Can you tell when you have lunch?" he asked. "I can't figure this schedule out at all."

102

"I'm not sure," I said, trying to read my schedule. "I think I can have it now if I want."

"It's too early for lunch," he said. "It's too early for breakfast."

"I guess later then," I said. "I don't know. I don't understand anything. They call their teachers by their first names."

"The class applauded us when we walked into homeroom," Elliot said. "Standing ovation."

"How awful," I said.

"I think I'd better find my way to the gym," Elliot said. "Maybe I'll find you later."

"I hope so," I said. It hurt terribly when he walked off. I stood in the hallway for a few moments and then started walking, anyplace, trying to find something to do, something that looked familiar. A mean-looking teacher and rows of well-used desks, with kids chewing gum and looking bored. Notes and whispers. This school didn't even smell like a real school. All the rooms were light and airy, and just barely looked institutional. But it was mostly the noise level that got to me. There was no one teacher droning on, while the kids sat in silence. There was talk and laughter, and a sense of total participation.

I hated it. It wasn't home and I hated it. I hated everything about it. I hated knowing I was supposed to call the teachers by their first names, and that they trusted me enough to let me wander about for two of those mods, getting familiar with what seemed so alien to me. I hated Edward Albee. I hated Lacy for fitting right in. I hated not knowing where Kenny and Melissa were. I hated April for being where she belonged. Where I belonged too. I was so full of hate, I barely recognized Paul when I bumped into him.

"Thank God," he said, and held me before I started charging off again. "A familiar face."

"Where are you going?" I asked him. I didn't even whisper. Nobody seemed to care if you stood around in the hallway talking. There were other groups of kids doing it all over the place.

"I don't know," Paul said. "They just told me I could wander now. So I'm wandering."

"This is a nightmare," I said.

"Let's wander together," he said. "Maybe it won't be so scary that way."

"I get to do this next mod too," I told him as we peeked into classrooms.

"Poor kid," Paul said. "They have me down for something real then. Math, I think."

"I never thought I'd miss those stupid rules," I said. "But I crave alphabetical order."

"You know what really stinks?" he said. "By the time we have all this worked out and it's starting to feel comfortable, we'll be back at Southfield. And then we'll have to adjust to all those stupid rules all over again."

"You're right," I said. "That really stinks."

"I think that's the library," Paul said, and sure enough it was. There were real books there, on real shelves, and it was the first room that looked like what it was supposed to be. I sank into a seat with a sign of gratitude. Paul did the same.

Pretty soon a couple of kids came over to us. We began talking in animated whispers about the

Shaft and just what was happening and why. I even recognized one of the kids, a girl who had been in homeroom and English with me. Her name was Irene and she was wearing a bright red shirt. Irene in a red shirt. It wasn't much, but it was a start.

Irene explained that our free time really wasn't intended to be spent wandering around but in various independent projects. Of course most of the projects had been decided on already, and the kids were hard at work on them. We'd have to decide what we wanted to concentrate our efforts on. She was doing an independent study to determine if marital status affected voting patterns. She doubted it did, but it seemed worth finding out. She even handed Paul and me questionnaires to fill out for her survey.

I spent my next mod right where I was, feeling a little sense of security at the library. It was a good thing I did, because my next mod was French, and that was a shocker.

I'd been preparing myself for the reality that French here would be taught differently from French at Southfield. I wasn't unhappy with that. It would probably be more conversational here, and I liked that idea. My accent could sure use some improvement.

But what I wasn't expecting was to enter a classroom of eleven- and twelve-year-olds. I felt like a fool walking in.

"*Bienvenue,* Becca," the teacher said. "*Voici votre leçon de français.*"

I knew enough French to understand what she said, but not enough to answer.

"Are you sure?" I asked. "I mean, everybody looks so young."

"*Nous commençons le français très jeune, ici.*" Then she had pity on me. "We start studying French at a much earlier age here," she said in English. "We estimate that this is the level of your French."

Suddenly I lost all desire to take French. "There aren't any French classes with kids my own age?" I asked.

"Of course there are," the teacher continued. "But they're all on college level. Advanced college level. I'm sure you'll feel much more comfortable here."

"I don't want to take French then," I said. "Do I have to take French?"

"No, of course not," the teacher said. "You don't have to do anything at Merwin. Education should be a joy, not an obligation."

"I don't feel joyous," I said. "I think I'll go back to the library. Maybe I'll do some independent study in French."

"That's an excellent idea," the teacher said, but I sure didn't stick around long enough to discuss it. I just ran back to the library, back to the only security I knew. Maybe it would be lunch soon. Maybe this would all be over soon. Maybe I could make it through the day.

I stayed in the library until it was probably lunch time, and nobody said a thing to me about it. I joined everyone I could find in the cafeteria and mostly listened to Lacy rave about the school.

"They treat you like adults here," she said. "I can't believe it."

106

It was nice one of us was happy. I kept looking around for Kenny and Melissa, but I couldn't find them, and nobody else had seen them. I had an awful feeling I knew what that meant, but I just couldn't believe it, and nobody even suggested it.

Things improved in the afternoon. The classes seemed more like classes. There was chemistry, and you couldn't muck around too much with that. History wasn't exactly structured, but I enjoyed the free flow there. They were debating ideas, and I could understand that.

And gym was a lot better than at Southfield. We had a choice between tennis and racketball. I didn't have anything to change into, so I just watched, but that was okay too, because I finally spotted Melissa. She was in the hallway, staring in.

"Where were you?" I asked, walking over to her. "Where's Kenny?"

"I really can't talk," she said. "Please, Becca."

"Okay," I said. "But is Kenny here?"

"No," she said. "Look, I'm late, and I've got to find the main office or something."

"Don't worry about being late," I said. "They don't worry about anything here. It's really weird."

"Let me go, Becca," Melissa said. "I really do have to go."

"Okay," I said, and I let go of her hand. "Is Kenny coming later?"

"Kenny isn't coming," she said, and before it sank in, she was halfway down the hall.

TEN

Elliot's maid did take us home, but I had her drop me off at Kenny's apartment building instead. I knew I had to see him, and waiting until the schoolday ended practically drove me crazy. Much as I wanted to press Melissa for information, I knew it might cost me my friendship with her, a price I wasn't about to pay. So I stared at my nonexistent fingernails, pretended to pay attention, and tried not to scream.

I buzzed Kenny's apartment, and over the intercom I could hear a scratchy version of his voice. He buzzed the door open, and I went in. Kenny's apartment was on the second floor, so I walked up the stairs. He had the door open for me.

"What happened?" I asked, starting to shake with anger. "Where were you?"

"I was in school," he said. "Sit down, would you, Becca? And stop looking at me like that."

"Like what?" I said.

But Kenny didn't answer. Instead he took my jacket and hung it up. I looked around his apartment. It was loaded with oversize furniture left over from his parents' old home. The entire room looked overstuffed.

Kenny sat down on the sofa, and I sat down opposite him on a chair. No passionate embraces. Not until I had some answers.

"Becca," he began, but then he just gestured helplessly with his hands. "Becca, I don't think you're going to understand."

"Try me," I said, understanding all too well already.

"It's been horrible," he said. "For me and for Melissa. Her mother was after her all weekend long to get her to write those apologies. And she wouldn't do it. Her father and mother started fighting really bad, and for a little while it looked like Uncle Joe was going to walk out."

"Because of this?" I asked.

"It's as good an excuse as any," Kenny said. "They've been having problems."

"But Melissa was at Merwin today," I said. "I saw her this afternoon."

"I guess she won then," he said. "She fought hard and mean. I've never seen Melissa like that. But she wasn't going to apologize. She just didn't think she'd done anything wrong."

"And you think she did?" I asked shrilly.

"No, of course not," Kenny said. "Look, Becca, Melissa won because her father was on her side. I don't think Uncle Joe really cares about the constitutional issues. He just hates Malloy's guts."

"Don't we all."

"I guess Aunt Phyllis realized she was outnumbered. Or maybe she didn't want her marriage to end that way. If you say Melissa was at Merwin, Aunt Phyllis must have finally caved in."

I didn't much care for the caved-in image, but

at least now I could understand why Melissa had looked so miserable. I wished she had let me help. "What about you?" I asked. "Now that you've told me about Melissa."

"It wasn't a great weekend for me either," he said.

"It wasn't a great weekend for anybody," I said. "None of this has been fun, Kenny. Now what happened?"

"Give me a chance, will you?" he said. "You're just waiting to jump on me. I'm not the enemy, you know."

I wanted to say I was sorry, but I had a feeling I'd be angry at myself later if I apologized. So I kept quiet.

"They found out about the suspension at Burger Bliss," Kenny said. "That I was involved. And the manager told me he couldn't have me working there while it was unresolved."

"But that's crazy," I said. "They have dropouts working there."

"Oh, yeah," Kenny said. "It's fine if you're a dropout. It's if you're in trouble with school that there are problems. Company policy. Nothing personal. It was all explained to me very logically."

"But you told me you worked on Saturday," I said.

"I did work," Kenny said. "I told them I intended to apologize, and would be readmitted on Monday, and they let me work. They did me that favor. Against the manager's judgment. He was feeling charitable that day, or so he told me."

"But then you could have started school at Merwin on Monday," I said. "And then you'd be

110

going to school, so you wouldn't really be in trouble, and they should have let you keep your job."

"That thought occurred to me," Kenny said. "I told Mom that even. And she pointed out that if I was working at Burger Bliss twenty hours a week, it kind of implied that we didn't have the money for me to go to some fancy private school."

"But it's only for one semester," I said.

Kenny sighed. "I called my father," he said. "I tried to explain it to him. And all I got from him was a list of his outstanding bills. Business is rotten, and he has all these debts from the good old days when we all lived in a nice big house and pretended to be a happy American family. I told him what the tuition was and he laughed."

"Oh, Kenny," I said.

"It wasn't fun," he said. "Dad had a lot of strong opinions about a son who would even think about making demands like that when his life was in such shambles. He threatened to declare bankruptcy. He threatened lots of stuff."

"What about your grandparents?" I asked.

"I wasn't about to call Dad's family," Kenny said. "And Mom refused to let me call hers. They don't have that much money anyway, and now that Granddad's retired, things are tight for them."

"So you gave in," I said.

"I didn't have a choice," Kenny said. "Not really."

"There's always a choice," I said. "If you're willing to look hard enough, there's a choice. You just didn't think it was worth the effort."

"Becca, the world is not as simple as you think it is," Kenny said. "Money counts for a lot more

111

than you give it credit for. This is the real world where you don't get everything you want, and sometimes you lose battles, and sometimes you have no choice but to give in. It's about time you realized that."

"I don't realize anything," I said. "Except that you sold out. When things were at their worst, you just sold out. Like some kind of coward."

"What would you have had me do?" he cried. "If I didn't apologize, and I couldn't go to Merwin, I would have been stuck without school, without a job. Without anything. Becca, I want to get back the things I lost when Dad walked out. I want the house, the cars, the boat. I want the security. I have to get into a good college, and I have to get a scholarship *and* work like hell, and no place in America would have taken me seriously if I applied with a chunk of my junior year missing."

"But there's more to life than cars and houses," I said. "Boats. So you don't have a boat anymore. Most people never have a boat. Most people don't have security either. Not real security. Look at your grandparents."

"I look at them all the time," Kenny said. "Them and my father and his bankruptcy, and my mother who works at a job she hates because she's determined to live in this town so I can go to a good public school. We should have moved years ago, after Dad left, some city somewhere, but Mom wouldn't let us. This school system is too important to her. For me. For my future. So we live in this crappy apartment with its cardboard walls, and Mom's social life is nonexistent, unless you count the passes her boss makes at her, and we save every damn penny we can get our hands on. For the future. For my future. That's not something I can let go of easily."

"If you have all those pennies saved up, I bet there was enough money for Merwin," I said.

"Forget it," Kenny said. "You don't understand. You don't understand a single goddamn thing, do you, Becca? You just fight your holy wars, and the hell with understanding."

"I understand," I said slowly. I wanted him to hear every word. "I understand that you knew all this Saturday night when you came over, and you didn't tell me any of it. I understand that you tried to get me to go to bed with you, and you made me tell you over and over again that I loved you, and all the time you knew you were going to go back to Southfield. All those hugs and kisses and I love yous, and you weren't honest with me for a single moment. You're a liar, Kenny, a cheap rotten little liar and you disgust me."

"Take your jacket and get out," he said. "I'm sick of you and your self-righteousness. If you really cared about people, you'd understand. You might even forgive if understanding was too hard. But you'd just rather feel all noble about yourself, like being righteous meant being right. It doesn't always, you know."

"The last thing I need from you is a lesson in morals," I said. "Your only morality is money and getting what you want."

"That's so easy for you to say," he said. "You always get what you want. And money doesn't mean a thing to people who have it. Take Elliot.

Or Paul. They don't have to worry about anything. There's always someone to pick up what they've dropped, to fix what they've broken. God, I hate them all."

"I'm not rich like them," I said. "You hate me too?"

"You're rich enough," he said.

"So you do hate me," I said. "Why have you been dating me then? Or why don't you date someone who really is rich? Marry young. Have her family put you through college."

"That's not a bad idea," Kenny said. "I'll think about it."

"You sicken me," I said, finally getting up. "You're really disgusting. It's just amazing you could be related to Melissa. Melissa who fought with her mother to get what she knew was right."

"Melissa has her own fights," Kenny said. "Sometimes she wins, sometimes she loses. But her situation isn't the same as mine."

"I want my jacket," I said.

"Then get it yourself," Kenny said, but he got up from the sofa and walked over to the closet. He took the jacket off the hanger and tossed it to me. For a moment I stared at him, and then I put it on.

"You'll need better manners than that to marry money," I said.

"I'll take lessons," he said. "Maybe ask Paul's mother for pointers. She's done it often enough."

I might have smiled except for the waves of anger that were still sweeping through my body. Instead, I put on my jacket.

114

"'Bye, Becca," Kenny said, standing by the closet.

"Wait," I said. "You didn't write anything either. For the *Shaft*. Like April."

"I know," Kenny said. "All I did was sell a few copies."

"So what did you say you did?" I asked.

"I told Malloy I drew all the cartoons," Kenny said. "It seemed to me Lacy was willing to give up credit for them, so I took it."

"But Malloy was angriest about the cartoons," I said.

"Tell me about it," he said.

"Was he rough on you?"

Kenny was silent. "I've had better days," he said finally.

"You didn't have to take credit for the cartoons," I said. "You could have picked something innocuous."

He shrugged. "I figured the innocuous stuff would be in demand later," he said. "In case you guys lose."

"We won't lose," I said. "And you'll be so sorry then, Kenny."

"I couldn't take that chance," he said. "I've watched my father play double or nothing all my life, and it's not my game. The odds just aren't good enough for me."

"It isn't double or nothing," I said. "Not if you're right. If you're right, the odds are on your side."

Kenny smiled. "Maybe," he said. "I'll have to take your word for it, though."

I could hear the TV go on in the apartment

next door. Kenny was right. The walls were made of cardboard. I wondered how much of our fight the neighbors had heard, and if they really cared. Probably not. I was probably the only person who cared. I couldn't even be sure Kenny did anymore.

"I've got to go," I said.

"All right," he said.

I walked over to the door and put my hand on the knob. This was the moment he was supposed to rush to my side, kiss me, admit he'd been wrong, and promise he'd tell Malloy that in the morning. This was the moment when his love for me should convince him to fight the good fight. To care about his battles, and not just give up when it looked like he might lose. This was the moment when he was supposed to realize that cars and houses and boats were nothing compared to principles—and losing me.

So I stood by the door and waited for Kenny to come to his senses. Only he stood by the closet and just stared at me. Eventually he broke his glance and looked away, toward the windows, toward anyplace where I wasn't.

Feeling like a fool, I opened the door and left.

ELEVEN

Maybe there was more to my life than pain those next few days, but I don't remember it. The only thing I seemed to be aware of was pain and loneliness.

At school the only people I felt any closeness to were Elliot and Paul. It was hard to talk with Elliot, though; he was jittery and bounced around rather than sitting. I'm not sure he went to any of his classes; we had a couple in common, but I almost never saw him.

"This place is so crazy," he told me during a free mod. "All this spare time."

"Well, you're supposed to work in it," I said.

He smiled at me. I'd noticed Elliot smiling a lot lately, but they were odd smiles, self-protective ones. "I don't want to work," he said. "There's nothing to work on."

"That's okay," I said. "They don't care."

"Dad cares," he said. "He's after me all the time. How am I doing? Am I happy? Do I like it here?"

"Your father cares a lot about you," I said. "You know that."

"He's suffocating me," Elliot said. "He hasn't been this bad since Mom died."

"He's worried," I said. Actually, it sounded kind of nice. My parents were still maintaining a quiet distance from me.

"He had a lot less to worry about when he worried a lot less," Elliot said, and then he smiled again. "Excuse me, Becca, but I think I'd better get moving. I get the jitters when I sit down for too long."

"Okay," I said, and watched him dance away. It felt like he was dancing into a different world, one I couldn't follow him into. He had been distant and alone when his mother died, and it had taken years for him to return to normal. I just hoped he'd rebound faster this time.

Jittery as he was, at least Elliot hadn't shut himself off from me the way Lacy and Melissa had. Of course Lacy and Melissa had shut themselves off in very different manners. Lacy was simply so happy she was unbearable.

"I just can't get over it," she told me a couple of days after we'd started at Merwin. "This place is all my wildest fantasies about what a school should be. All the freedom and respect. Don't you just love it?"

I felt petty admitting I didn't, so I just nodded.

"And the kids here," she went on. "They're so terrific. So much more mature than the kids at Southfield. Oh, I know, you're from there, and I've loved being friends with you, but here there are just so many kids interested in the same things I care about. None of this gung ho football and school spirit, and who's going to win the

118

student council election garbage. Books count here and brains, and the teachers know it too, and it's just so terrific. I never knew I could be so happy. At least until I was an adult."

I tried hard not to sigh.

"Oh, come on," Lacy said almost harshly. "You can't possibly miss Southfield."

"Sure I can," I said. "That's why I'm taking them to court."

"Oh," Lacy said, sounding genuinely surprised. "I thought it was because of the holy constitutional principle."

"That too," I said, but I'd given up caring about principles. So what if my rights had been violated. I just wanted to go home.

"If you're so desperate to get back in, you can always apologize," Lacy said. "Kenny may have taken my cartoons, but I'm sure there's still something you can take credit for."

"How did you know about Kenny?" I asked.

"He called me," she replied. "To tell me the cartoons were now his. I told him he had my blessing. I can do better work than that anyway."

"How did he sound?" I asked.

"Like a broken man," Lacy said, and then laughed. "Honestly, Becca. He sounded like Kenny. A little sulky, but otherwise fine. If you want to know so much, why don't you call him?"

"I can't," I said.

"You mean you won't."

"I mean I can't," I said. That was one principle I still believe in.

"You look awful, you know," Lacy said. She looked terrific. I think she'd bought an entire

119

new wardrobe in the past two days. "Do you sleep at all anymore?"

"Sure," I said.

"You've put on weight," she said. "You look like you don't care about anything anymore."

"Maybe I don't," I said, but I knew that was a lie. I cared about staying angry at Kenny. Maybe not much more than that, but that was still important.

"I hope this won't sound heartless, but I really feel like I'm making a new life for myself here," Lacy said. "A real life, the one I should have had all the time. And frankly, Becca, you're a bit of a drag."

That I knew only too well.

"So shape up," she said. "Okay?"

"Sure," I said, knowing that shaping up was not in my immediate future.

When I saw Melissa later, she at least had the grace not to be happy. But she was in a state of total isolation, worse even than Elliot's. She was almost zombielike.

"Don't you think we should talk?" I asked her one day after school. "I'm worried sick about you."

"The only person you're worried sick about is yourself," she said.

"Melissa!"

"It's true," she said. "Not just of you, but of everybody. That's the one thing I've learned from all this. That we're all really alone, and our pain is our pain alone."

"What about your father?" I asked. "He's been on your side."

"Just because it wasn't my mother's," Melissa

said. "They look for things to fight about, and this one was a gem."

"That can't be true," I said.

"Becca, you always assume you know everything," Melissa said. "You always think you have vision into everybody's life. But you don't. There are things you couldn't begin to understand."

"Wait one second!" I shouted, not caring that we were walking in the center of town and were surrounded by people. "What do you mean by that, Melissa? Do you really think I'm that uncaring? Do you blame me for all this?"

"Maybe I do," she said, and stood absolutely still. "Maybe if you hadn't talked back to Mr. Malloy, we'd all be at Southfield, a little sadder, but basically normal. You were the one who forced the issue. You were the one who said we shouldn't apologize. Do you have any idea what Kenny went through, what kind of hell you put him in? Do you even care?"

"We make our own hells," I said. "Kenny certainly made his."

"Sometimes I think you have no heart," Melissa said.

I couldn't speak. I just stared at her, my mouth gaping.

"You have all those fine principles," Melissa went on. "Truth and justice and the American way. But there isn't a drop of compassion in your soul."

"That's not true," I said.

"Look at yourself someday," Melissa said. "Look really hard. I don't think you'll be too happy with what you find."

"I hate you," I said, and then I shouted, because Melissa had started to move on. "Do you hear me, I hate you!"

She didn't even look back.

So that left only Paul. Paul, whom I'd never liked. Only that didn't seem to matter anymore. It wasn't that I liked him now, because I still didn't, but he and I were in the same boat, and we were the only ones who seemed to be rowing in the same direction. And that made me feel as close to him as to anybody else I knew.

There seemed to be a tacit understanding that since I was just temporarily at Merwin (I hoped, I prayed), there was no need for me to develop any independent projects to occupy my spare mods. Ordinarily that should have made me happy, but it just made me feel more like a nonperson. Even school didn't expect anything from me. I didn't feel like taking on anything that wasn't demanded of me, but that left me with an enormous amount of free time and not enough energy to employ it well. So I just sat in the library and pretended to read books and magazines and newspapers. A lot of the time Paul sat with me and pretended to read alongside. I stared at him occasionally, while he was looking down, and tried to think what it was he felt he'd lost.

"Do you see April?" I asked him one day.

He grimaced slightly. "No," he said.

I felt a small surge of gladness. "Because she apologized?" I asked, pressing my luck.

"I don't think so," Paul said. "I've been thinking about that a lot lately. It might have been a factor, but I can't be sure."

"What do you mean?" I asked.

Paul rubbed the back of his neck absently. I wondered if he was as knotted up there as I was. "I understood why April apologized," he said. "She really never did feel part of the *Shaft* group. She joined because I did. April loves to follow."

I nodded.

"So I felt bad when she got into the same jam as the rest of us," he said. "It didn't seem fair. April didn't contribute a blasted thing to the *Shaft* except her looks."

I thought about April's blondness and smiled.

"When she apologized, it wasn't the same as when Kenny did," Paul said. "I can understand why Kenny felt he had to, and maybe he was right, but at least there's an argument to be made that he shouldn't have. Kenny didn't join just because you were there. He was really excited about the idea at first. He was determined to work on it. He didn't end up doing very much, but Kenny's better at starting things than he is at keeping them going."

Part of me still wanted to defend Kenny, but I told myself that was just a reflex and kept quiet.

"Anyway, after April told me she was going to apologize, and we worked out what she should do, we went out together," Paul said. "I think to prove to both of us that what she did was okay. Only all she did was apologize to me. She wanted to know if she should call up everybody, you and Elliot and everyone else, and apologize to them too. She was just so damned sorry about everything it really got on my nerves.

"So then I started thinking about April," Paul

123

continued. "She does apologize a lot. She was sorry she didn't understand jokes, and she was sorry she hadn't had the same teachers I'd had, and she was sorry she didn't like the same movie or TV show or book. It got to the point where we were both scared to express an opinion because she'd end up apologizing."

"April seemed nice," I said. "But not too bright."

"She's probably a lot smarter than any of us ever gave her credit for being," Paul said. "If she just took some of that energy she spent on apologizing and used it on her mind instead, she might really be something."

"So that's why you're not dating her anymore?" I asked. "Because she apologized all the time?"

Paul looked at me carefully. "I don't really like you," he said. "And as far as I can tell you don't really like me, and that's just fine. But even when I didn't like you the most, I always had to like the way you faced things. I don't think I've ever seen you run off from a battle. Not in third grade when the teacher sent you to the principal's office, and you kept shouting that you were innocent, or in junior high when Lonny McKay kept teasing you in homeroom and you finally just kicked him."

"In the shins," I said. "I hurt him too."

"You sure did," Paul said. "We teased him for months after that. You gave him quite a black and blue mark."

"I'd like to kick Malloy now," I said.

"Get in line," Paul said.

"You fight your battles too," I said. "I've never thought otherwise."

"I'm not so sure," Paul said. "I've watched me

124

not stick up for things I believe in. I've watched me compromise on things I really didn't want to compromise on. I've watched me give in, make the right move, not stand up for things. And I've always known you would fight. That didn't make me like you any more. Probably less. But on this one, it's been good for me. I know you're miserable, and I can imagine what you're going through because of Kenny, but it's really been good for me. Because I won't give in as long as you won't. Which has nothing to do with whether I like you or not. I'm just using you as my backbone."

I laughed. "It's funny to think I have any backbone left for you to use," I said.

"I think about us a lot," Paul said. "The seven of us, I mean. Who's going to come out of this better, and who's going to come out worse."

"Tell me," I said. "I'd love to know."

"Lacy's the obvious one," he said. "She's almost pretty now, have you noticed? So happy it's scary. And Melissa is miserable and shutting herself off from everybody, so she's obviously coming out worse."

"What about Kenny?" I asked.

"He's about the same, I think," Paul said. "You may not agree, but I just don't see much change there. Elliot is a lot worse. I'm really worried about him. April is essentially unchanged, unless something is going on that she's not showing."

"How are you doing?" I asked.

"I'm doing well," he said. "I'm not happy, and it's no great thrill to me that you're the only person I can really open up to. But I can feel myself getting stronger because of this. I can feel myself learning how to get in control, but in a positive way. I know I manipulate people well, but this is something else, and I like it. It's making me smarter, and I like that."

"What about me?" I asked. "How am I going to come through?"

Paul looked at me thoughtfully. "I don't know yet," he said.

"Oh, come on," I said. "You have an opinion for every occasion. You must have one about me."

"It certainly hasn't made you any more likable," he said, but he smiled, and I smiled back. "This whole business, it's sort of like this school. I really hate this school, you know. I really like structure."

"I miss structure," I said. "But I'm still not sure I like it."

"The thing is they really believe you get what you put into it at a school like this," Paul said. "I don't think they're right, but that seems to be their philosophy. You work during your free mods, you get something out of them. You waste the time, you waste the possibilities."

"But what does that have to do with me?" I asked.

"It's like this," he said. "I'm getting something out of this whole mess because I'm determined to. I've picked getting stronger. Melissa's picked losing. Maybe not consciously, but that was her decision. If her parents split up, she'll blame all this for it. And if she tosses away friendships, then she'll blame this. Everything. She's determined to be as miserable as possible. And Elliot's using it as an excuse for panicking. I think he's wanted to panic for a long time now, but never really had a reason to before."

"And I haven't decided yet?" I asked.

"Unless I'm wrong," Paul said, arching his eyebrows. "Which, of course, I never am."

"Yeah, sure," I said.

"If you want it to work for you, it can," he said. "You still have that much control. Or if you want to use it as an excuse for everything, you can do that too."

"But if I don't have the energy to decide?" I asked.

"That's a decision too," he said. "Don't you know that yet?"

"I'm learning," I said. "Just give me time."

TWELVE

The next Monday, Melissa didn't come to school.

I didn't want to know why, but Paul told me anyway. "Her mother called my mother," he said during a spare mod. "To gloat, I think. Melissa's apologized."

"I don't believe it," I said. "The way she fought her mother about it?"

"I guess the fighting got to be too much," Paul said. "I wanted to talk to her, but her mother made it very clear she didn't want any of us near Melissa."

"I bet Kenny talked her into it," I said.

"All I know is that she took credit for what she'd written," Paul said. "In case you're still keeping track."

"I'm surprised you're still here," I said. "I bet you go next."

"I'm not going anywhere," he replied. "Except to my next mod."

"I'm sorry I said that," I said. "I'm just upset."

"Things must have been bad for Melissa," Paul said. "All that anger must have worn her down."

"I'm not going to bomb her house," I said. "Or even spit at her mother. Okay?"

128

"Okay," he said, but we both knew nothing was okay. I couldn't remember the last time anything was.

On my way home I made a list of what I'd gained from all this, and what I'd lost. Under gain, I put pain, aggravation, fury, and weight. Under loss I put Kenny, Melissa, education, and peace of mind. Loss was an easy winner.

Dinnertimes at my family are usually harried. Dad and Mom frequently bring work home to do and are impatient to get to it. Occasionally they have late meetings and skip supper at home altogether. Abby and I are both accustomed to making our own suppers and eating them on our own schedules. The past week we seemed to have gotten together even less than usual. I was convinced it was because my parents were avoiding me. When we were in the same house together we hardly spoke. So a few conveniently timed late meetings made sense to me. I'd avoid me if I had a choice.

That Monday night, though, maybe because it was the start of a whole new week, we were all at home. I got home first, so I started the cooking. I made a stew. It felt good cutting the vegetables up, and the onions were a convenient excuse for a few tears. I wasn't feeling great by the time everybody got home, but I was reasonably all right and certainly willing to give family togetherness a try.

"Well," Dad said as he ladled himself some stew. "This certainly is a pleasure. All of us eating together, just like a normal family."

"We are a normal family," Mom said, taking some salad. "This meal looks delicious, Becca."

129

"Thank you," I said. I'd set the table nicely too, figuring we could all use a pleasant dinner. Good china, fresh tablecloth.

"We ought to do this more often," Dad said. "We don't see enough of each other. We ought to have one meal a week just like this, good food, nice-looking table, all of us together. What do you say?"

"It sounds lovely," Mom said. "But it's so hard to coordinate our schedules. We're all so busy."

"I'll say," Abby said, taking some stew. "I have band practice, and drama club meetings, and debate club meetings, and music lessons. Plus schoolwork."

"No wonder I never see you," Dad said. "Lately it feels as if I never see anybody outside the office. The McHugh case is taking a lot more time than I thought it would."

"How's it going?" I asked, nibbling at the salad.

"Not so great," Dad said. "Things should work out before our court date, but right now the other side is just delaying and delaying, and that isn't helping us any. The sooner we go to court, the better."

I wanted to ask him if a court date had been set for my case, but I didn't want to bring it up at supper. So I just nodded.

"It looks like we might get the women's study program going next year," Mom said. "I think we've licked just about all the problems."

"That's good," Dad said. "I know you've been worried about the administration."

"We've finally gotten Dean Robinson on our

130

side," Mom said. "And his opinion carries a lot of weight. God knows we need a good women's program."

"I'd love to study women's stuff," Abby said. "I wish they offered it at school."

"Melissa apologized," I said. I hadn't meant to, but it slipped out.

"I know," Dad said. "Her mother called the office to tell us she was no longer participating in the suit."

"It's her mother's fault," I said. "She was really rough on Melissa."

"She was doing what she thought was best," Dad said. "Even if you don't agree with her."

I wished I were back in the kitchen peeling onions. "It's just four of us now," I said. "Will that affect our chances?"

"It shouldn't," Dad said.

"I saw Kenny at school today," Abby said. "He asked after you, Becca."

"That was nice of him," I said. "Was he happy that Melissa was back?"

"I didn't ask him," Abby said. "You're still mad at him?"

"I'm not mad at him," I said. "Not the way you mean. He betrayed our cause, and I'll never forgive him."

Dad looked like he was going to choke. "Wait a second, Becca," he said, putting down his fork. "Kenny was under a lot of financial pressures, and he made a reasonable decision. You sound like some kind of revolutionary, getting ready to shoot the traitor."

"I don't approve of what he did," I said. "Or Melissa, or April. If that makes me sound like a revolutionary, I'm sorry."

Nothing tasted good anymore. We all just played with our food, in ever heavier silence.

"Guess what," Abby said brightly. "They announced the cast for the junior play. Mike Daley is going to student direct, and Jan Schultz got the female lead. I think Dave Epstein is starring."

"The junior play?" I said. I'd forgotten all about it.

"I think Jan'll be really good, don't you," Abby said. "You've always said she could really act."

If I'd been there, I would have tried out. Even doing something offstage, props or publicity, would have been fun. I would have liked heading the publicity department.

"Do they have class plays at Merwin?" Mom asked.

"No," I said, swallowing hard. I didn't want to cry at the dinner table. It was bad enough I was full of self-pity; I didn't want everyone else to know I was.

"They probably have something," Dad said. "Maybe if you asked one of the teachers . . ."

"They don't, Dad," I said, although to be perfectly honest, I didn't have the slightest idea. It just didn't sound like the kind of thing they did at Merwin. "They're not big on school activities at Merwin."

"That's terrible," Abby said. "I think activities are the best part of school."

"Just as long as your grades don't show that,"

132

Dad said, chuckling. He started eating his stew again. I think for a moment I hated him.

"We get to do a play with the sophomores," Abby said. "In January. Maybe I'll try out."

"You ought to," Mom said. "I'm sure you'd do well."

"Really?" Abby asked. "Do you think I'd get a lead?"

"It depends on what the play is," Mom said. "And if you're right for any of the roles."

"Maybe I should be an actress," Abby said. "Like a movie star. Do you think I could be a movie star?"

"I think you'd be a wonderful movie star," Dad said. "Abigail Holtz. I can see your name in lights right now."

"Wow," Abby said. "What do you think, Becca?"

"I think you'd make a great movie star," I said, staring at the window. My mind was on the committees for the junior play. Even if everything were resolved tomorrow, I doubted they'd let me chair a committee. They probably wouldn't let us do anything important at Southfield ever. I wondered if they were going to be nicer to Melissa, since she apologized before the case went to court. Melissa was as active in school activities as I had been. She'd go crazy if they didn't let her do stuff. Especially now that she wouldn't have the *Shaft* to keep her busy.

It really must have hurt her to go back. I didn't exactly forgive her, but if my parents had been acting the way hers had, maybe I would have apologized too. Maybe.

133

"It certainly sounds like we're all keeping busy," Mom said, which was sort of a lie, since I hadn't said anything about doing anything. "I think that's good."

"I know it's good," Dad said. "I'd go crazy if I didn't have a half-dozen things going on at the same time. Blame it on a Type A personality."

"I love all my different clubs," Abby said. "I can't wait until next year when I'm eligible to run for club office. I want to be president of the drama club someday."

"What do you want to be, a politician or a movie star?" Dad asked.

"Nowadays you can be both," Mom said.

"Guess what else happened," Abby said. "At school? We had this assembly, and Mr. Deacon was supposed to make the introductions, only he forgot who he was introducing, and he just stood on the stage and looked so dumb. We all laughed at him. Remember Mr. Deacon, Becca?"

"Of course I remember Mr. Deacon!" I said. "I've only been away from school for a couple of weeks."

"I thought maybe you hadn't had him since freshman year, so you might have forgotten him," Abby said.

"I haven't forgotten any of them," I said. "But to be perfectly honest I don't see what's so funny about Mr. Deacon getting embarrassed onstage."

"It was funny," Abby said. "That's all. He looked dumb."

"So he looked dumb," I said. "We all look dumb occasionally. I bet there are times you look dumb too, Abby."

"What are you getting so mad about?" she asked. "I just thought you'd be interested."

"It isn't my school anymore," I said. "I don't want to hear anything about it anymore."

"What am I supposed to do?" Abby asked. "Just never talk about school anymore?"

"In front of me, yeah," I said. "You could learn to keep your mouth shut, couldn't you?"

"Why should I?" she shouted. "All I've been doing lately is keeping my mouth shut. This is practically the first time since you stopped going to school that I've even mentioned it. It's driving me crazy not talking in front of you."

"Some drive," I said.

"Mom!" Abby cried.

"Becca," Mom said sharply.

"I'm sorry," I said. "But you don't seem to understand how much it hurts me to hear about what's going on at Southfield. I want to be there so bad it hurts. It hurts all the time. I hate it at Merwin. I hate it that Kenny and Melissa went back, and I can't because it would be wrong to. I hate everything and everybody."

Mom shrugged her shoulders.

"I especially hate you!" I screamed at her. "You and your sighs and your shrugs. I'm sorry my fight isn't sacred enough for your tastes. It's a shame I didn't get suspended for protesting nuclear power or saving whales. Next time I'll check my cause with you before I do anything about it."

"Becca," Mom said, but I'd already stormed out of the dining room and run to my bedroom. I thought about flinging myself onto my bed, and

135

having yet another crying fit, but instead I sat down on the floor of the closet and balled my body up so it took as little space as possible. The quiet darkness helped. I knew at some point I'd have to come out, and after that I'd have to apologize, but for a little while at least I felt secure.

There was a knock on the door. "Go away," I mumbled.

Whoever was there didn't hear me because the door opened. "Becca?" I heard Mom call. "Becca, are you in there?"

"I'm in the closet," I said.

"What?" Mom said, and turned on a light. "Becca, where are you?"

"In the closet," I said more clearly.

Mom walked over to the closet and pulled open the door. She stared at me in horror for a moment, and then she started laughing.

I turned away from her.

"I'm sorry, honey," she said, still laughing. "But if you could just see yourself."

"I didn't tell you to come in here," I said.

"I came here because I love you," she said. "Sweetie, do you think you could get out of the closet, so we could talk?"

"Why should I?" I asked, and buried my head between my knees.

"Okay," Mom said, and sat down on the floor of the closet next to me. "Let's talk in here."

"You don't have to coddle me," I said.

"That's just what I have to do," Mom said. "That's just what I haven't been doing, and I've been wrong."

136

I lifted my head up, but I still didn't look at her.

"You weren't very nice to Abby in there," Mom said. "She's upset, but I talked to her, and I know she understands."

"Mom, it hurts!" I cried.

"I know, honey," she said, hugging me as best she could. "It hurts and I sure haven't been much of a help."

"You've been awful," I said, hugging Mom back. It felt so good to be in her arms.

"I've been very angry," Mom said. "Angrier than I should have been, probably. You were right. I did think you stumbled into your battle, and I did think it wasn't worth the pain you were subjecting yourself to, or the emotional and financial cost."

I shifted my body so we were no longer hugging. But Mom kept her arm around my shoulders.

"I believe in the things I fight for," Mom said. "And I pick my battles selectively. I've watched too many people throw themselves into one cause after another and drop them as soon as things got tough."

"I haven't dropped anything," I said.

"You certainly haven't," Mom said. "Maybe I needed to have you prove that to me."

"I'm getting awfully tired of proving things," I said. "Why can't you take things on simple faith?"

"From now on I will," Mom promised. "I can see the pain you've been through. I know you haven't been happy at Merwin, and I know how miserable you must be because of Kenny and

Melissa. And I know I haven't been much of a help."

I looked down at the closet floor. "I never thought it would hurt this much," I said. "I'm not sure—if I'd known from the very beginning—I would have done any of it."

"Sometimes fights choose us," Mom said. "We don't always have the luxury of picking them. I seem to have forgotten that."

"I'm sorry I had to remind you," I said.

"I'm sorry you've had to learn it so early," Mom said. "I want everything to be perfect for you and Abby."

"Next year maybe," I said.

"Next lifetime is more like it," Mom said.

"I shouldn't have picked on Abby," I said. "I know that. I'll talk to her."

"Please do. Today was the first day Abby seemed herself again. She's been so upset since all this began. She idolizes you, and to see you in trouble and unhappy has really confused her."

"I think confusion is my middle name," I said. "Maybe if I talk to Abby we can make sense out of all this together."

"I love you," Mom said, and she hugged me again. "And I'm really very proud of you."

"You are?" I asked.

"I am," she said. "For hanging in there and sticking up for your rights. And for the *Shaft*."

"You read it?" I asked hesitantly.

"I did," she said. "It took me a while to get past that silly cartoon, but then I did read it. And it was very good. Much better than any of the issues of the *Sentinel* I read."

138

"Oh, thank you, Mom," I said, and this time I hugged her.

"I'll make a deal with you," Mom said. "I promise I'll be more supportive and let you know just how much I respect you and love you if you promise to get out of this closet. I'm getting an awful leg cramp."

We both laughed. "You have to get out first," I said. "You're blocking my way."

"Not anymore," Mom said, and helped me up.

THIRTEEN

Things got better after that.

For one thing, I apologized to Abby. It was a little scary. I was used to being in control of that relationship; she was the one who usually did the apologizing. But this time I was the one who was flat out wrong, so I was the one nervously knocking on the door, begging for admittance.

Abby, at least, wasn't sitting on her closet floor. She was on her bed, a box of tissues by her side, staring at the wall.

"Abby, I'm really sorry," I said.

"It's okay," she said. "Mom talked to me about it."

"It isn't okay," I said. "I've been horrible lately. I don't know why you've put up with me this long."

"I know it isn't your fault," she said, turning around to face me. Her eyes were red, and that made me feel even worse.

"Not all of it is my fault," I said. "But I could have been nicer. Braver maybe. I feel so sorry for myself all the time."

140

"I feel that way lots of times," she said. "It goes away."

"Has it been rough for you at school?" I asked. "Are they still teasing you about me?"

"Not much," she said. "Mostly nobody seems to care."

"Terrific," I said, surprised at the bitterness in my voice. "You see, Abby? That's just what I'm talking about. I should be glad for you, and instead I'm moping about me again."

"I love you, Becca," Abby said.

"Oh, Abby, thank you," I said. "I'm so glad you're my sister."

And that made things a lot better.

I still didn't much like Merwin, but I knew that I felt ill at ease there because it was temporary. Assuming we won, and I was refusing to assume otherwise. One good thing, though, was that I knew that the four of us who were still there were going to remain there. Lacy was having too good a time to leave, and Elliot was too strange to make any decisions on his own. And Paul wouldn't leave unless I did, and I sure wasn't about to. I missed Melissa's friendship, but not having her there looking like a zombie was kind of a relief. And I was getting used to missing Kenny; that was just becoming part of me.

It was November already, and I knew that one way or another a decision was coming soon, and that helped too. When I got a call from Jim Jordan telling me he'd like me to come in for a pretrial conference, I told him that would be just fine. We set a date for that Thursday.

I can't say I was excited about the meeting, but it seemed like a positive step, and I was getting bored being negative all the time. I was almost at the point where I wanted to come up with some independent study to fill up those empty mods. Only I was torn between doing an in-depth study of freedom of the press and never having anything to do with freedom of the press again. It was just the sort of conflict to keep me from doing anything, which was probably why I picked it.

I never did go back to French—that was just too much for me—but I took out a French novel from the school library, and I began reading it with the constant help of a French-English dictionary. It was hard going, but I liked that. I was starting to feel as if my mind had gone the way of my fingernails.

I also started running. I wasn't up to doing two miles a day, like Abby, but I'd start out with her early each morning, and I'd do what I could while she kept going. She tried hard to be nice about it, but I could tell what intense pleasure it gave her to be able to do something better than I could. And that brought out the competitive spirit in me, so each day I did a little bit more. Competition and the desire to take off the ten pounds I'd put on because of all the craziness were great incentives.

And once my life started fitting into a pattern again, I started feeling like myself. Maybe the patterns weren't the ones I was used to, but they'd do for the time being. And if they were the patterns I'd have to learn to live with, if we actually did lose and I had to stay at Merwin, then

I'd make the most of those patterns. Run, read French, study some issue that didn't make me want to choke every time I thought about it. Worry about Elliot. Talk to Paul with less and less wariness. Start thinking about making decisions. Know I wasn't going to die no matter what happened.

I took the train into the city Thursday at noon, having left Merwin early for the purpose of consulting with my attorney. They wouldn't have cared, but I loved having such a classy excuse. I could have skipped the morning, but we were talking about *Long Day's Journey into Night* in English, and I wanted to be there. I stayed on to read my French novel, and then left, by cab, to the local train station.

I got a bite to eat at the terminal, and then took a bus uptown to Dad's office. It was a trip I'd made many times before, usually with Mom and Abby. I know the route, and I felt comfortable making it on my own. Comfortable, and a little nervous about what Jim Jordan was going to be saying to me. But it was a healthy sort of nervous, because I knew it was bringing me closer to the end of all this and the start of whatever was going to be started. And I was curious to find out.

"Becca, hi," Mrs. Lardner said. She'd been the receptionist for as long as I could remember, fussing over Abby and me and saying how cute we were, and how much we'd grown, sort of like an aunt.

"Hi," I said, smiling at the memories. "How're things going?"

"Fine," she said. "But your father's been a

bear lately. Don't get into so much trouble next time, all right? It's terrible for his disposition."

"I'm never getting into trouble again," I said. "Scout's honor. If Dad's free, I'd love to say hello."

"He's meeting with a client," Mrs. Lardner said. "But I'm sure he'll be through by the time you are. So why don't you just go into Mr. Jordan's office first. He's expecting you."

"Okay," I said. I would have liked to touch base with Dad, have him escort me to Mr. Jordan's office, remind everybody that I was the boss's daughter, but I could hardly ask Dad to leave a client just to play the proud papa. Especially if I was causing him to behave in bearlike ways. So I just followed Mrs. Lardner to one of the smaller offices and knocked on the open door.

"Come in, Becca," Mr. Jordan said. "Sit down, make yourself comfortable." I certainly tried after Mrs. Lardner had left. Just me and my lawyer. I tried to remember how nervous I was feeling so that when I was a lawyer and I had clients come in and sit down I'd be able to understand what they were going through, and not just sit there and read over some papers the way Mr. Jordan was doing.

"I'm sorry, Becca," he said, putting the papers down on his already cluttered desk. "Just too damn much work. Your father must complain about the same thing."

"All the time," I said, shifting my weight in the chair.

"I love the work," he said. "But sometimes I wish there were a little less of it."

"We'll be off your back soon," I said, trying to sound sympathetic.

"Hell, you're the least of it," he said. "You guys are fun. I'm sure it's been awful for you, but from a legal standpoint, it's been quite interesting. I wish all my cases were as interesting."

"I'm glad you're having a good time," I said.

Mr. Jordan stared at me, then he laughed. "I'm sorry, Becca," he said. "I'm nervous as hell, because you're Phil's daughter. I must be sounding like a damn fool."

"I'm nervous too," I said. "Partly because I'm Phil's daughter."

We both laughed. "Fair enough," he said. "Now why don't we start like sensible people and see if you have any questions."

"I would like to know if the trial's going to be very soon, Mr. Jordan," I said.

"Jim," he said. "Call me Jim."

"Okay, Jim," I said, and it didn't feel so weird because I'd had three weeks' worth of practice calling my teachers by their first names. Something to be grateful to Merwin for.

"The trial is set for next Tuesday," he said.

"Tuesday!" I said. "That soon?"

"It's taken long enough," Jim said. "Don't you think?"

"Tuesday," I repeated. "Are you ready?"

Jim laughed. "I sure as hell hope so," he said. "If I'm not, we're all in big trouble."

I tried to laugh.

"I've been doing my research, and I've met with everybody. You're my last interview," he said. "I think we have an excellent shot at winning on Tuesday. It wouldn't surprise me if you were back at Southfield within a week."

"Wow," I whispered. "What's going to happen?"

"You know the basic strategy," he said. "We're claiming that your First Amendment rights were violated by Malloy and the school board."

"What about the fact we sold the paper on school premises?" I asked.

"Things would be easier if you hadn't," Jim said. "But I've gone through the school rulebook, and there doesn't seem to be any specific rule against selling newspapers or magazines on school premises. And the legal precedents are on our side."

"We never even thought about it," I said. "It just seemed like the sensible place to do it."

"So Paul told me," Jim said.

"Will the trial take very long?" I asked.

"I don't think so," he said. "We should be able to do it all in a day, if we're the first thing on the calendar."

"A day," I said, wondering if the judge would have any idea how important that day would be in our lives.

"You should know that since this isn't a jury trial, it's going to be a lot looser than what you've seen on TV," Jim said. "The other attorney, the judge, and I have had a pretrial conference to plan out the trial, so we all have a good idea of what's going to happen."

"That sounds like collusion!" I said.

"Hardly," Jim said, laughing. "But it is a time-saver."

146

"I guess," I said. "Does Dad do that sort of thing?"

"All lawyers do," Jim said. "Any other questions?"

Part of me wanted to ask what would happen if we lost, but I knew Jim couldn't give me the answers to that one. So I just shook my head.

"I have some questions for you if I may."

"Sure," I said.

"I'd like to know if you'd object to testifying," he said. "Let me explain that if I call you as a witness, the school board lawyer will have the chance to cross-examine you, and she may not be very nice. I don't know just how nasty she'd be willing to get, since you are an appealing kid, and the judge might not like it if she ripped you to shreds, but it's a possibility you have to be aware of. She won't be as nice to you as I'll be, in any event."

"Then why should I testify?"

"For a couple of reasons," Jim said. "First of all, I'd like the judge to see what a nice kid you really are. And I think our case will be a lot stronger if a couple of the kids had a chance to explain why they got involved with the *Shaft*, and what the suspension has done to them. There are constitutional issues in this case, but it won't hurt for Judge Denning to be reminded that there are kids' futures involved too."

"A couple of kids," I said. "Which ones?"

"You and Paul," Jim said.

"Why us?" I asked.

"I don't have a helluva lot of choices," he said. "I thought about having Melissa testify, but I'm just as glad I don't have to make that decision. She might have been fine, or she might have broken down on the witness stand, and not ever gotten the pieces put back together."

"This has been hardest on her," I said. "Of all of us, she's the one who's had it the worst."

"You're probably right," Jim said. "Anyway, Melissa eliminated herself from competition. I can't ask Lacy. She's so wild about Merwin she'd probably just sing its praises. Or tear down Southfield, which seems to be the other thing she most enjoys doing."

"Lacy's a little weird," I said. "But she's happy now, and that's good."

"It's fine for her, but not for us," Jim said. "At least not in terms of having her testifying. And I don't think Elliot could get through testifying without having a drink. We don't need him drunk."

"Oh, come on," I said nervously. "It's not that bad."

"Yes, it is," Jim said. "I know the symptoms. It's that bad. But that's his problem. His and his father's."

"All this did that to him," I said. "The suspension. It's Malloy's fault."

"I don't think so," Jim said. "I didn't know Elliot beforehand, of course, but I'd be surprised if this began just because of the suspension. I imagine there have been problems for a long time now, and this just forced them out into the open."

I wasn't sure he was right, but I wasn't sure he was wrong either. I just knew I grieved for Elliot and I hated Malloy and I couldn't really separate those feelings.

"Fortunately you and Paul should make excellent witnesses," Jim said. "Paul's self-assured, but he doesn't come off cocky."

"That's only because you don't know him," I said.

"Judge Denning doesn't know him either," Jim said. "So that's to our advantage. And you seem to have a good grasp of the legal issues of this case. You understand the principle involved."

"Sometimes," I said. "Sometimes I just get so scared and angry I forget there are principles. I just want to kill."

"But that's the side I know won't show when you're testifying," he said. "If you're willing to testify."

"I guess so," I said. "Does Dad think it's okay?"

"He does," Jim said. "I sure as hell wasn't going to ask you to if it weren't all right with him."

"You curse a lot," I said.

Jim laughed. "You may not believe this, but I'm on best behavior," he said. "Usually every third word out of my mouth is a curse."

"It's been every fourth word," I said.

"Sorry if it offends you," he said.

"It doesn't," I said. "It's just something I notice because I don't curse."

"You don't?" he asked. "Not at all?"

"I think there are plenty of words in the English language without picking curse words," I said.

Jim stared at me, and then he burst out laughing. "You worked for the scummiest magazine I've ever had the pleasure of reading, and you don't even curse?" he asked.

"I wrote the think pieces," I said stiffly. "Not the scummy stuff."

"I see," he said, but I could tell he was trying not to laugh. "Well, it's an advantage that you don't curse. One less thing to worry about when you testify."

"Did I sound horrible?" I asked. "Puritanical? Stuffy?"

"Maybe a little," Jim said.

"I used to be much nicer," I said. "Before all this happened. You know how you said Elliot had all those problems all along, and this just brought them out into the open?"

Jim nodded.

"It's been the same with me," I said slowly. "It's like sometimes I would be mean about people, but kind of lightly, like I'd make jokes that weren't very nice, only now I get really angry and I don't make jokes anymore. I used to think April was just silly, but after she apologized, for a day or so I really hated her."

"That's understandable," Jim said.

"But I still hate Kenny," I said. "I may always hate Kenny. And I really have to work at it to feel any sort of compassion for Melissa. I used to think I was a sympathetic person, but I'm not sure anymore."

"This has been an ordeal for you," Jim said. "And I really think the only thing you learn about yourself in an ordeal is how you'll behave in one."

"You think I'll go back to being a nice person when this is all over?"

"I don't think you ever stopped," Jim said. "You're just hurt and confused and scared."

"I'm sorry," I said, looking down. "This isn't your problem."

"That's okay," Jim said. "Will it help any if I tell you how proud of you your father is?"

"Dad?" I said, trying to keep the surprise out of my voice.

"He thinks you're wonderful," Jim said. "The way you've been battling, and refusing to give up no matter what. He's in here every day, checking to see what's new with the case, go over possibilities with me. He's even threatened to run for school board, to have a chance to fire Malloy."

"He never told me that," I said.

"That's because nobody behaves well during an ordeal," Jim said. "Including parents."

"How are you during one?" I asked him.

"The pits," he said cheerfully. "I curse all the time."

"Sounds good," I said. "Maybe I'll try it."

It felt fine to be laughing again.

FOURTEEN

The thing that surprised me most about the courtroom was it looked just like courtrooms on TV.

I figured it would look different, since I don't
trust much of what I see on TV. But it looked like
a stage set, the judge's chair behind that platform
desk, and the witness chair next to it, and desks
for the lawyers in front of the audience section.
There was even a court reporter.

Thinking of it all as a set added to the unreality.
Feeling light-headed, I held onto Mom as we made
our way into the audience seats. We sat as a
group; Paul sat next to me. It was comforting
having him there. Elliot sat two seats away, next
to his father. He was shaking so much his father
must have noticed, but Mr. Silvers didn't say anything about it that I could hear. Lacy was seated
between her parents, and she looked as if she
didn't have a care in the world. I guess she didn't.
If she lost the case, she'd just get to stay on at
Merwin, which certainly wouldn't bother her.

Abby had asked to come, but Mom and Dad decided she ought to go to school. It was just parents and us, no siblings allowed. The parents were

there in full force, though; even Paul's stepfather made an appearance.

"Dad wanted to come too," he whispered to me
as we waited for the judge to make his appearance.
"But it was just too far away, and he couldn't
make it."

I tried smiling at him, which felt strange. I'd
smiled at Paul more in the past month than I had
in the previous eight years, but I still wasn't
comfortable being sympathetic with him. I guess
he sensed that because he turned away from me.
So I tapped him gently with my hand and whispered, "You're going to be fantastic."

"So will you," he said, and smiled at me. I guess
it felt strange to him too, since he looked embarrassed, and then we both laughed. Someone's
parent shushed us, and we immediately fell quiet.

Dad was sitting next to Jim at the lawyer's
table. Jim looked relaxed, but I know Dad well
enough to recognize his tension symptoms. He
was tapping on the desk with his finger, and
jiggling his left leg, and whispering what seemed
to be last-minute instructions to Jim, who nodded
and whispered back occasionally.

The lawyer for the school board was a woman,
which I still thought was a dirty trick. It didn't
seem fair that their side, which was so blatantly
wrong, should have a woman lawyer, when we,
the forces of good, were represented by two men.
She looked like a nice enough woman too, in her
thirties, with well-cut hair and a brown wool suit.
I checked my outfit again nervously: a plaid skirt,
white blouse, and a blazer. I'd worried more about

what I was going to wear to court than I usually did for a date.

"All rise! The honorable Judge Denning presiding!"

So we rose, and I tried to get a good look at the man who was going to be deciding my fate. He was tall, with thin gray hair and thick glasses. He had on a black robe, just like a TV judge, and when he sat down I really did feel like I'd stumbled into a made-for-TV movie. *Becca Holtz: Victim!* Or *Becca's Triumph!* Something with an exclamation mark for sure.

Jim called his first witness, who turned out to be a psychologist. Because of the pretrial conference, he didn't have to make an opening statement.

The psychologist gave all his credentials, which were awesome, and then Jim asked him if reading pornographic material would be injurious to high-school-age students.

I wasn't thrilled that Jim was labeling the *Shaft* pornographic, but then I decided that made sense. If we acted like it wasn't, then the other side would keep hammering away at us until we admitted it was, even if it wasn't. This way we just conceded the point and proved it wasn't important.

By the time I'd worked all that out, the psychologist was almost finished explaining that in our sexually active society pornography on the level of that in the *Shaft* wouldn't be harmful. The other lawyer, whose name was Ms. Buckman, didn't have any questions. I sure would have,

154

but maybe that meant she wasn't competent. A comforting thought.

Then Jim called out "Thomas Rice," and up walked this pimply kid who couldn't have been more than fourteen. He looked vaguely familiar, but I couldn't place him.

It turned out Thomas went to Southfield, where he was in ninth grade. I tried to remember if Abby had ever mentioned him, but I was too curious about why he'd been called by our side.

"Tell me, Tom," Jim said. "Have you seen the *Shaft?*"

"Yes, sir," Tom said, scratching at one of his pimples.

"Hot stuff, huh?" Jim said.

"It's okay," Tom said. "I've seen better."

I thought I heard Paul huff, but I didn't dare turn around to check.

"You've read better?" Jim asked.

"Oh, yeah," Tom said.

"Like what?" Jim asked.

"*Dudes* is pretty good," Tom said. "But my favorite is *Hot Pussy.*"

A few people snickered.

Jim handed Tom copies of magazines and asked if those were the ones he meant. Tom looked them over, turned bright red, and said they were. Jim asked that they be marked as evidence. Judge Denning agreed, and casually flipped through the magazines. He turned bright red too.

"Where do you buy those magazines?" Jim asked Tom.

"At Gerber's," Tom replied.

155

"Gerber's," Jim said. "Is that a local newspaper store?"

"Yeah," Tom said. "It's right around the corner from school."

"Do many of your friends read *Dudes*?" Jim asked.

"Sure," Tom said.

"And have you ever seen copies of magazines like *Dudes* and *Hot Pussy* in high school? In the actual building?"

"Sure," Tom said. "Different guys bring them in. We check out the pictures in the locker room or in the cafeteria."

"Have you ever gotten in trouble for reading those magazines in school?" Jim asked.

"No," Tom said. "I guess I would if I read them during English or something, but as long as the teachers don't know, they don't care."

"That's all," Jim said. "Thank you, Tom."

So then Ms. Buckman got up. I watched anxiously, because if she was rough with Tom, she'd be murder with me.

"Tell me, Tom," she said, sounding nice enough, "have you ever bought a copy of *Dudes* on campus? In the high school building, for example."

"Not *Dudes*," Tom said. "No, ma'am. But Gerry Moskowitz sold me three copies of *Hot Pussy*. In gym. I looked them over in the locker room to make sure he hadn't cut out the good stuff, but they were all okay, so I bought them for two dollars. Each."

Ms. Buckman looked flustered. I figured that meant two points for our side.

Jim called up another boy, this one with braces on his teeth. His testimony was almost the same as Tom's. Ms. Buckman didn't ask him any questions.

I figured Jim would call Paul and me next, but instead he said he wanted to reserve his last witnesses until after Ms. Buckman had presented her case. Ms. Buckman agreed to let him do it, so I guess they had discussed it before. It still seemed like collusion to me.

Ms. Buckman started off just the way Jim had, with a psychologist. This one also had credentials as long as the Bible. Only he said pornography was terrible for kids to read, and that something like the *Shaft*, which held teachers up to sexual ridicule, could damage a student for years to come.

That made me feel rotten. First of all, everything he said disagreed with everything our psychologist said, and that just didn't make any sense. But there was always the possibility their psychologist was right, and we really had hurt someone.

I wanted Jim to rip that psychologist to shreds, but he hardly asked any questions. It was our psychologist against theirs. They both seemed equally important, so I didn't know how the judge was supposed to decide which one was right. I had a feeling the judge's prejudices might enter into it.

A psychologist wasn't enough for Ms. Buckman. She called in a priest next. The priest explained that he was on the committee of an antipornography clergy group, and that they were fighting pornography in all its forms. Including high school underground newspapers.

"The *Shaft* is despicable," the priest said. "It doesn't matter that children wrote it. Children can be hurt by it just as much as if adults had written it. More, perhaps, because if children think other children are responsible, they might think it's acceptable for them to do these very things."

I thought about Abby and for a moment felt nearly sick with guilt. But then I calmed down, and I realized that Abby wasn't about to find herself a bear to make love with. And it seemed okay to me if she worked on a magazine like the *Shaft*, assuming she didn't get in trouble because of it. I wasn't ashamed, even if they did bring in a psychologist and a priest to tell me I should be.

Jim asked the priest a few questions to find out what he regarded as being pornographic. The priest seemed to think everything short of Walt Disney was questionable, and even Disney wasn't all it once was. That made me feel a lot better.

Which was a help, because the next witness was Miss Holdstein. There she was, looking just the way she had the last time I'd seen her, when we'd all been called away from her history class. Open-toed shoes, pearls around the neck, brightly flowered dress on her tall, gawky body.

She explained who she was, and then Ms. Buckman asked her if she'd seen the cartoon in the *Shaft*. Miss Holdstein looked at it and said she had.

"Where did you see it?" Ms. Buckman asked.

"At Southfield High School," Miss Holdstein said. "I noticed several students laughing during

158

one of my classes, and I confiscated a copy to see what was amusing them so."

Up until then, I really hadn't thought about Miss Holdstein ever seeing a copy of the *Shaft*. Mom had been mad at me because of Miss Holdstein, but I figured she could get through all this without actually seeing it. Or if she did see it, it would be because Malloy had shown her a copy, and then it would have been his fault. I pictured Miss Holdstein getting a copy because she took it from some kids, and that was awful.

"Did this cartoon upset you?" Ms. Buckman asked.

Miss Holdstein squinted at the cartoon. "It did," she said.

"What did you do when you saw it?" Ms. Buckman asked.

"I did nothing," Miss Holdstein said. "I simply continued teaching. But as soon as the class was over, I went to the teachers' lounge and I wept."

I looked down on the floor. I never meant for Miss Holdstein to weep. I didn't even know there were tears in that body.

"That will be all," Ms. Buckman said. "Thank you."

Only then Jim got up. "Tell me, Miss Holdstein," he said conversationally, "have you ever made a student weep?"

"What?" she asked.

"Have you ever had a student cry in your classroom because of something you said to him or her?" Jim asked.

Miss Holdstein looked flustered. "I don't know," she said.

"In all the years you've been teaching, you've never once made a student cry?" Jim persisted.

"Maybe once," Miss Holdstein said.

"And do you think there might have been times when a student didn't cry in front of you, for the same reasons you didn't cry in front of the students, but then left the classroom and wept as you did?" Jim asked.

"Objection!" Ms. Buckman said.

"Sustained," Judge Denning said.

"I have no further questions for this witness," Jim said.

So Miss Holdstein left the witness chair. I still didn't feel good that she had wept.

Next came Mr. Malloy. I didn't care one bit if we'd made him weep. He looked just the way he had, too, only meaner, if that was possible.

Lacy stuck her tongue out at him, really quick, and then looked completely innocent. I doubt that anyone else saw her, but it helped me relax a little.

Ms. Buckman went over it all with Malloy, how he'd gotten a copy of the *Shaft*, and how he'd called us all into his office, and how fair he'd been giving us a chance to apologize right there and just serve a short suspension, but how obstinate and rude we'd been, until he realized that we simply didn't feel any remorse about what we'd done.

"Was it then that you decided to extend the suspension further?" Ms. Buckman asked.

"Yes, it was," Malloy said. "I would not have these insolent pornographers attending my school. There is entirely too much disrespect for teachers

160

and administrators at Southfield High School, and an example had to be made of them."

"Since the suspension, three students from the *Shaft* staff have returned to Southfield," Ms. Buckman said. "Isn't that right?"

"Yes, they have," Malloy said. "They wrote letters of apology and were readmitted immediately."

"Have they complained to you that your treatment of them was unduly harsh?" Ms. Buckman asked.

"Absolutely not," Malloy said. "As a matter of fact, the mother of one of them came to me and thanked me for taking such a firm stand."

Melissa's mother, I decided, but I knew that wasn't fair. It could have been April's mother. Or Malloy could have made the whole thing up.

But Jim didn't ask him about that. Instead he asked if drugs were a problem at Southfield.

"We are concerned about drugs, yes," Malloy said.

"Isn't it true that last March four boys and a girl were found smoking marijuana on school grounds by one of the teachers?" Jim asked.

"Uh, yes," Malloy said. "I believe that did happen."

"Were those students punished?" Jim asked.

"Yes, sir, they certainly were," Malloy said, looking very proud of himself.

"In what way were they punished?" Jim asked.

"Well, it was quite a while ago," Malloy said. "I can't absolutely remember."

"Is it true that each was suspended from school for three days?" Jim asked. "And then readmitted without further constraints?"

Malloy licked his lips nervously. "Drugs are a very serious problem among today's teen-agers," he said.

"They certainly are," Jim said. "Possession of marijuana is illegal in this state. Did you know that, Mr. Malloy?"

"Yes, of course," Malloy said.

"So for committing a crime these students were suspended for three days," Jim said.

"It's more complicated than that," Malloy said. "Believe me, if I had my way, those students would be in jail today. But the school board refuses to face up to its responsibility in these matters."

"Do you regard writing and distributing an underground newspaper as a more serious offense than the possession of marijuana?" Jim asked.

"No, of course not," Malloy said.

"But your punishment was more severe," Jim said.

"I had to set an example," Malloy said. "These students had to be taught that they couldn't get away with things any longer."

"Has it worked?" Jim asked.

"What?" Malloy asked.

"Have there been any new problems at Southfield High School since the suspension?" Jim asked.

"There are always problems," Malloy said, trying to laugh.

"Is it true that last week a student was suspended for calling a teacher by an obscene name?" Jim asked.

"Yes," Malloy said.

"And wasn't there a fistfight in the cafeteria two weeks ago?" Jim asked.

"Yes," Malloy said. "But of course there will always be incidents."

"Yes," Jim said. "I imagine there always will be. The student who was suspended for calling the teacher an obscenity. How long was he suspended for?"

"Two days," Malloy said.

"And the students who got into the fistfight?"

"They weren't suspended," Malloy said. "They each got a week's detention."

"That will be all," Jim said. "Thank you."

Ms. Buckman looked as if she might want to ask some more questions, but I think she was mad because of what Malloy said about the school board. She did work for them, after all.

It turned out Malloy was her last witness, so then Jim called up Paul. I gave his hand a squeeze, and he winked at me. He looked good walking up to the witness stand, and he took the oath, and said his name nice and clearly.

I wasn't positive what Jim was going to ask him, but it was hard concentrating when I knew I was going to be next. I was starting to get sick to my stomach instead. Still, Jim seemed to be asking stuff about how the suspension had affected Paul, how he had to go to a new school, and how it might affect his chances at college.

I stopped listening and checked out the impression Paul was making. It seemed to be a good one. He didn't sound like a wiseguy, and he didn't sound angry. He explained about Merwin and how different it was from Southfield and how hard it

163

was making the adjustment, especially since we all hoped it would just be a temporary one. And he explained about how important your junior year was when colleges were checking out transcripts. The judge seemed to be paying attention, and Ms. Buckman was writing notes furiously. That didn't make me feel any better.

Jim didn't take long with Paul, and then Ms. Buckman got up. "What did you write for the *Shaft?*" she asked him.

Paul looked panicked. "I worked on a lot of things," he said. "We all contributed to everything."

"But surely you worked on one article in particular," Ms. Buckman said.

"Yeah," Paul said, not looking self-confident anymore. "There was an article on the quality of teaching at Southfield. I wrote that one."

"You refused to tell Mr. Malloy that when he asked you, didn't you?" Ms. Buckman said.

"I didn't tell him," Paul said.

"Was there any reason why you refused to volunteer that information?" Ms. Buckman asked.

Paul thought for a moment. "We were scared," he said. "And we didn't know what Mr. Malloy intended. We didn't think it was right for some of us to get into more trouble than others because they'd worked on one specific thing. And we'd decided not to have our names on any of the articles just because we all did work on everything together."

"So you chose to be disrespectful when you saw Mr. Malloy," Ms. Buckman said.

"We didn't mean to be disrespectful," Paul said.

"Tell me, Paul," Ms. Buckman said, "we've heard a lot from you about how rough all this has been in terms of your education and your college plans. So we know you're upset it's all happened. But are you sorry for any other reason? Do you feel any sense of remorse?"

"Yes," Paul said. "I am sorry. I really am."

"Thank you," Ms. Buckman said.

I thought Jim might ask Paul some more questions, but instead my name was called. I thought I might faint, but I managed to make my way to the witness stand. I passed Paul, and I could see he was sweating. I tried breathing deeply, but it all felt so strange. Especially when I had to put my hand on the Bible and take the oath that I would tell the truth, the whole truth, and nothing but the truth. Then I announced my name and sat down. I did look at Dad, sitting at the counsel's table, and he half smiled at me.

"You were one of the seven students suspended from Southfield High School, weren't you, Becca?" Jim began.

"Yes, sir, I was," I said, hoping I sounded okay.

"And since the suspension you've been attending the Merwin School?" he continued.

"Yes, sir," I said.

"Has it been easy for you to go to a new school?" he asked.

"No, sir," I said. "It's been very hard. The two schools are really different."

"Were you a good student at Southfield?" Jim asked.

"I was an honor student," I said.

"And did you belong to any clubs?" he asked.

"I was a member of the debate club," I said. "And the French club. And I was a member of the student council."

"It sounds like you kept busy," Jim said. "Have you joined any clubs at Merwin?"

"No, sir," I said. "It's hard getting involved someplace when you don't know if you'll be there very long."

"Do you want to go back to Southfield?"

"Oh, yes, a lot," I said.

"Enough to apologize for your participation on the *Shaft*?" Jim asked.

"No," I said. "Not enough for that."

"Why not, Becca?" Jim asked.

Jim had told me not to sound like a know-it-all and not to sound angry. Just explain how I felt about things and keep it short. "My father's a lawyer," I said, looking at Dad. "And he always taught me that rights were rights, that it didn't matter how old you were or where you worked or what color you were, that your rights were the same as anybody else's. And I feel that I have as much right to work on a newspaper as anybody else, and if they don't have to apologize, neither should I."

"Thank you, Becca," Jim said. "Ms. Buckman?"

I knew better than to hope she wouldn't have any questions. I just hoped I could answer them without getting too upset.

"With all those clubs, I'm surprised you had time for the *Shaft*," she said.

I didn't know what to say, so I kept quiet.

"Why did you join the *Shaft*?" she asked.

166

"Because I didn't like the school newspaper," I said.

"Oh," Ms. Buckman said. "They didn't carry cartoons like that one?" and she showed me Miss Holdstein and the bear.

"No, ma'am," I said.

"I can certainly understand why you'd want to work on another newspaper then," she said.

I kept quiet.

"So you're not sorry enough to apologize," Ms. Buckman said.

"No," I said.

"Are you sorry at all, Becca?" she asked.

There was a part of me that wanted to say no, I wasn't the least bit sorry. But the funny thing was I knew that was a lie. Paul might have said he was sorry because that was the expedient thing to say, but I was going to because it was the truth.

"Yes, ma'am," I said. "I am sorry."

"But not sorry enough to apologize," she said.

"I'm not sorry that way," I said. I wanted to scream.

"Very well," Ms. Buckman said. "That will be all, Becca."

"I have one more question," Jim said. "Becca, in what way are you sorry?"

"I'm sorry I hurt Miss Holdstein's feelings," I said. "I really am."

Jim smiled. "Thank you, Becca," he said, and all of a sudden I was free to leave.

I tried to sit down in our row, but before I could edge my way down the aisle, I knew I was going to throw up. So I just said "excuse me" and left the courtroom. I made it through the doors and managed to find someone to ask the location of the nearest ladies' room. Fortunately it was nearby, because the instant I saw a toilet stall, everything started to come up. I made it just in time.

The toilet stall reminded me a lot of my closet, and I had no desire to leave it. I stayed in the ladies' room for as long as I could, washing my face with cold water, and then I left and looked for a water fountain for a long time before I finally found one. I took a long drink of water and thought about going back into our courtroom. Instead I found a bench and sat absolutely still for a few quiet moments.

I knew I had to get back to the courtroom before they sent bloodhounds looking for me, so I reluctantly got up and walked back. There were plenty of empty seats in the back, so I took one rather than make a disturbance going back to our row. I did see Mom turn around and spot me coming in. She smiled at me.

It took me a moment to figure out what was going on, and then I realized Jim was making his final statement. Dad had discussed that with me a little the night before. Jim got to go last, to answer any arguments the other attorney might have come up with.

"Age should not be a factor when it comes to freedom of the press," Jim was saying. "A high school student should have the same right to print his opinions as a high school teacher. We cannot expect our young people to respect a legal system that makes one set of rules for them

168

and another, less stringent set, for adults. The Constitution guarantees equal rights for all, and that's all these students are asking for. Thank you very much."

"Thank you, Mr. Jordan," Judge Denning said. "And you, Ms. Buckman. In today's schools, discipline is an ever-increasing problem. There must be times when a teacher or a principal senses anarchy all around, and the desire to reestablish discipline must be very strong indeed.

"Nonetheless, freedom of the press is a guaranteed right, one that applies to all Americans. Students should not be suspended for exercising their constitutional rights. I therefore rule that the plaintiffs be readmitted to Southfield High School tomorrow."

It was over. We'd won.

I wondered if I would ever breathe normally again.

FIFTEEN

Paul was right after all. It felt as weird to go back to Southfield on Monday as going to Merwin had been for the past few weeks.

We decided over a celebration lunch that we'd stay at Merwin through Friday, to give ourselves a chance to say good-bye to the friends we hadn't made, and to the teachers who hadn't taught us, and to the structure we never really found.

Mostly it was a chance to say good-bye to Lacy, who'd decided to stay on at Merwin.

"I think you guys are crazy to go back to Southfield," she said on Friday during our farewell lunch. "It's a horrible school."

"Maybe," I said. "But it's ours."

"Yours maybe, not mine," she said. "Malloy is going to make things miserable for you."

"I don't think he will," Paul said. "At least not as much as he might like to. The school board wasn't too thrilled about going to court and then losing. It doesn't reflect well on them. That's why they're not appealing. I think Malloy might be concerned about his job."

"I still think you're nuts," she said, which I

170

guess was her way of saying good-bye. Of course Lacy had always thought we were nuts, but now at least she was happy, so it was impossible not to be happy for her.

Saturday night I gave that victory party I'd promised Abby so long ago. Only it wasn't a big rousing party. I felt too strange to be rousing. Instead it was just Paul, Elliot, me, and our immediate families. Lacy decided she didn't want to come, and there was no one else we really felt like celebrating with. Jim Jordan came, of course, with his wife. Dad and Mom served a buffet dinner, and suddenly we found there were a lot of things to laugh about that hadn't seemed all that funny originally. We especially liked how Malloy sputtered on the witness stand. Dad acted out Malloy, and he did one fine sputter.

I walked over to Elliot at one point and found him standing by the kitchen door, sipping his coke.

"Let me have some of that," I said and took a gulp before he had a chance to complain. I nearly died. "How much booze is in that?" I managed to say.

"Not much," Elliot said.

"Not much!" I said. "Elliot, it's half rum."

"You're exaggerating," he said. "Rum just has a very strong taste."

"Elliot, you're drinking too much," I said. "Everyone knows that."

"I don't," he said. "I don't know that at all."

"You must," I said. "You haven't been at all like yourself lately."

Elliot gave me a strange look. "You never change, do you, Becca?" he said. "Always trying to run people's lives for them."

"I do not," I said. "Do I?"

"You sure do," he said. "If people don't conform to your image of what they should be, you really let them know it."

"If I do, it's because I love them," I said.

"The people you love might love you just a little more if you were easier on them," he said. "Let us make our own mistakes, lead our own lives. Just try it."

"You mean I should just stand by and not do anything while you turn into a drunk?" I asked.

"That's exactly what I mean," he said. "Because you might be wrong. I might not turn into a drunk. Or maybe I need to turn into a drunk before I can stop drinking. Or maybe I'll be happier as a drunk. There are a lot of possibilities that you refuse to acknowledge."

"Then how do I let you know I love you?" I asked softly.

Elliot shrugged his shoulders. "I haven't worked that one out yet," he said. "When I do, I'll let you know."

"I do care," I said.

"I know," he said. "A lot of people care. Maybe at some point that will make a difference."

So all I could do was hug him and hope he understood.

Sunday I spent very quietly, mostly in my room, trying to think. What Elliot said bothered me a lot, because I knew there were elements of truth to it, and that I didn't necessarily like what he'd told me about myself. I did stand in judgment. I did try to run people's lives. I felt better when I was controlling things, and I did try to control too much.

But it was all so complicated. How could I not tell Elliot we were worried about his drinking? That seemed to me to be immoral.

I tried to concentrate on that one for a while, but I knew it was just hiding what really concerned me, and that was Kenny. I had certainly tried to control his actions, and when he defied me, I just dropped him from my life. Melissa too, but I had a feeling she had done the dropping.

And that left me with no idea of how to act with them when we met at school. I just hoped when the moment arose, my instincts would tell me what to do.

"How do you feel?" Paul asked me as we walked to Southfield together the next morning.

"Terrified," I said. "Mostly that I'm just going to go in there and be so angry at everything and everybody that I'll never fit in again."

"I don't think we will fit in," Paul said. "Not the way we did before."

"That's not fair," I grumbled.

Paul laughed. "You still believe in fairness?" he asked.

"No," I said. "How do you feel?"

"Terrified," he said, and we both laughed. "It's kind of like a time warp. We've been running around in outer space, aging by the minute, and they've been staying at Southfield staying the same age. The same everything."

"I don't think that's how it works," I said. "I

think the ones in space are supposed to be the ones who stay the same age, while everybody on earth keeps on aging."

Paul smiled. "It depends on what space you've been running around in," he said.

"I know I feel older," I said. "And meaner."

"Did you ever decide whether you were going to profit from all this?" he asked. "Remember, likc we talked about?"

"Oh, I remember," I said. "I decided I couldn't decide."

"What do you mean?" he asked.

"There were too many pluses and too many minuses to count up properly," I said. "Maybe I'll know in five years."

"I'm better for it," he said. "I like being older and meaner."

We turned the corner and could see the high school a block away. "Paul, I feel really scared," I said. "Please, let's just stand here forever."

"Want to go back to Merwin?" he said.

"God, no," I said.

"Then it's forward march," he said, but he stood there with me, and we stared at the school. "It looks the same," he said finally.

"We probably do too," I said. "Except I'm fatter."

"You look okay," he said. "Better than you feel, probably."

"You mean we can fake them out?"

"Absolutely," Paul said. "If I didn't believe that, I wouldn't be here."

I took a few tentative steps toward the high

school. I felt breathless, like my heart was rushing out of my body, going into an orbit of its own.

"Race you there," Paul said.

"What?" I said.

"If we run we won't think," he said. "Bet I get there first."

"You're welcome to!" I said, but soon we were flying toward the school, the block vanishing underneath our feet. People were staring at us as we skimmed up the stairs to the main door, but that didn't matter. We would have been stared at no matter what.

We got to the front door and paused to catch our breaths. I looked at Paul, who was grinning back at me. "You know, I actually like you," I said, almost surprised to realize it.

"Yeah," he said between pants. "That's one of the pluses."

It was all I could do to keep from laughing out loud as we entered. Southfield still smelled like Southfield. Those miserable school smells I'd missed at Merwin were right there.

And my locker was still there, with its combination lock untouched. I walked over to it and, after getting it open, put my jacket in it.

As I did, Richard Klein walked up to me. "Hi, Becca," he said. "Welcome back. Congratulations."

"Thanks, Richard," I said. "It's good to be back."

"I don't know why," he said. "I would have thought you'd like that fancy school you all went to."

"Lacy did," I said. "The rest of us like plain old Southfield."

"The *Sentinel*'s missed you," he said. "I don't suppose you or Elliot would be interested in coming back?"

"You'll have to ask Elliot for yourself," I said. "But I don't think I am."

"Are you going to keep working on the *Shaft*?" he asked. "I guess you have the legal right to."

His question took me by surprise. It had never occurred to me that we had proved our right to publish a second issue of the *Shaft*. It sure would annoy Malloy if we did.

On the other hand, we'd lost a hefty portion of our staff, and other kids might be a little leery about working on it. It was worth mentioning to Paul, but I couldn't see us going ahead and doing it.

"Who knows," I said, just in case. "We haven't discussed it."

"If you change your mind about the *Sentinel*, let me know," he said. "Okay?"

"Sure," I said. "Is Melissa back on staff?"

"Didn't you know?" Richard said. "When she came back here, she resigned her membership in all the clubs. She was vice-president of the Spanish club, and she quit that too. I think she quit three different clubs, and that doesn't include the *Sentinel*."

"I didn't know," I said. "We haven't talked recently. Do you know why she did that?"

"She isn't saying," Richard said. "There are a couple of rumors going around, though. One is Mr. Malloy put pressure on her to do it."

"I can believe that," I said.

"But some kids say Mr. Malloy did just the op-

176

posite. Told Melissa she was welcome back, and he was going to let everybody know how proud he was of her because she dropped out of the lawsuit and came back here on his terms. Turn her into a bright and shining example. And Melissa responded to that by quitting everything."

"I can believe that too," I said with a shrug.

"They can't both be right," Richard said.

"It's possible neither is right," I said. "But they both sound plausible."

"Let me know if you hear anything," Richard said. "I'd be interested in knowing the truth."

I had my doubts that Melissa would be confiding anything in me, and even if she did, I didn't think I'd want to run over to Richard to tell him. So I half smiled and turned to another of the kids. There suddenly seemed to be a swarm of them around my locker, wanting to congratulate me and tell me they'd been on our side all the time. There was a moment when I really hated everybody, because they hadn't been there for me when I was in trouble. No committees, no petitions, no constant phone calls of sympathy and reassurance.

But then I made one of those snap decisions I hadn't thought I was still capable of. I decided if I hated everybody then, I might hate them for the next year and a half and that would be a waste of time and energy. So I chose to relax, and I talked with them as much as I could before the bell rang, and it was off to homeroom and the real world.

The morning went by in a whirl. I was behind in everything, and I knew I'd have horrible amounts of work to do to catch up with a month's worth of assignments. Even gym was different. We were off volleyball and onto basketball. The teachers all tried to act as if nothing had happened, but they didn't call on me, and I certainly didn't offer to say anything. I sat there and tried to absorb what was the same, what was different, and what I'd have to do to get back in the groove.

The only thing that really hurt was seeing Melissa and Kenny in some of my classes. We didn't make any moves toward each other, but I was so aware that they were there. It was small comfort that I knew they were every bit as uncomfortable.

Paul and I had made arrangements to have lunch together, but before we sat down at our table, I spotted Kenny and Melissa with some other kids at a table near the door. "I think we should talk to them," I whispered to Paul.

"This is kind of public," he said.

"I said talk, not scream," I said, and started leading the way through the mobs of curious kids. Kenny looked up and saw us coming.

"Oh," he said when we were standing by him.

"This was her idea," Paul said, gesturing at me. "But it's probably a good one."

"I just thought we should say . . ." I began, and then I realized I didn't have the slightest idea what to say. In all my fantasies the day before I'd failed to come up with a good approach to Kenny and Melissa.

"Yeah," Melissa said.

"So you guys won after all," Kenny said with a half laugh.

"Yeah," I said. "After all."

"Well," Melissa said.

"So we're back," Paul said, trying to make it sound conversational.

"We can see," Kenny said.

"We heard," Melissa said.

"Yeah," I said.

"Uh, how's Lacy?" Kenny asked.

"Fine," I said. "Very happy."

"That's good," he said.

"Well, we've got to get back to our table," Paul said. "Over there." He tried pointing with his tray.

"Okay," Kenny said.

" 'Bye," Melissa said.

"Yeah," Paul said, and he started walking toward the other end of the room. I followed him, surprised to find my hands were shaking.

"That didn't go the way I thought it would," I said to Paul when we returned to our table.

"It was a little strange," he said.

"I thought everything would be okay," I said. "But I was so angry. It never occurred to me I'd still feel so angry."

"You have every right to feel angry," Paul said. "I'm irritated myself, and I was never as close to them as you were."

"Will the anger go away?" I asked. "I'm so tired of being mad at people."

"Probably, with time," he said, and took a bite out of his sandwich. "There's one good thing about being an adult."

"What's that?" I asked.

179

"No food fights," he replied.

I dissolved in laughter. "Let's see if the food here is as bad as I remember."

"Worse," Paul said, his mouth full of sandwich. "Ah, Merwin, how I miss your charms."

I knew what was coming up would be even harder than dealing with Kenny and Melissa, and that was history with Miss Holdstein. I had thought about asking to be put in a different class, but that would have meant going through Mr. Malloy's office, and I wasn't about to ask any favors of him. So I made my way to history class, and tried to tell myself that bygones were bound to be bygones. At least I hoped so.

I sat down in my old chair, two seats back from Melissa's, and could hear the other kids buzzing about me. Elliot, three rows down, was staring out the window. I didn't feel like being conversational just then, so I opened my notebook conspicuously, and pretended to be reading last month's notes.

In walked Miss Holdstein, wearing her open-toed shoes, the pearls, and a vertical striped dress. She stood in front of the class and stared first at me and then at Elliot.

"I see Lacy is no longer with us," she said.

Elliot kept looking out the window, so I mumbled, "No." I'm not sure anyone heard me.

Miss Holdstein pursed her lips. "Very well," she said.

I could feel the other kids looking at me and at Elliot and then back at Miss Holdstein. I knew I was blushing, but that seemed to be the mildest of reactions. What I wanted to do was jump out the window and see if I could fly.

"I trust we are all adults here," Miss Holdstein said, and then she sat down behind her desk. "Today's topic is the Monroe Doctrine."

There was a communal breathing out.

"The Monroe Doctrine has certainly had its effect on our history," Miss Holdstein said in that drone I had almost missed at Merwin. "Do any of you have any thoughts on what that effect might have been?"

Everybody was quiet. I think we were all too involved still with the Malloy Doctrine.

"Surely one of you has some idea about the effect the Monroe Doctrine has had," Miss Holdstein said. "You have heard of the Monroe Doctrine, haven't you?"

There were a few titters, but still no hands.

Which was when I realized I had a lot of opinions about the Monroe Doctrine. And that's when my hand shot up, and I almost didn't care that everybody was staring at me, marveling at the return of my nerve.

Well, hell. You have to start somewhere.

ABOUT THE AUTHOR

As the daughter of a constitutional lawyer, Susan Beth Pfeffer grew up hearing about First Amendment cases, which served as an indirect inspiration for *A Matter of Principle*.

Her most recent books for Delacorte include *About David* (voted a Best Book for Young Adults by the American Library Association), and *Just Between Us* and *What Do You Do When Your Mouth Won't Open?*, companion volumes for younger readers and Junior Literary Guild Selections.

Susan Beth Pfeffer lives in Middletown, New York.